SHUT UP
AND DEAL

SHUT UP
AND DEAL

JESSE MAY

ANCHOR BOOKS

DOUBLEDAY

NEW YORK LONDON TORONTO SYDNEY AUCKLAND

AN ANCHOR BOOK

PUBLISHED BY DOUBLEDAY

a division of Bantam Doubleday Dell Publishing Group, Inc.

1540 Broadway, New York, New York 10036

ANCHOR BOOKS, DOUBLEDAY, and the portrayal of an anchor are
trademarks of Doubleday, a division of Bantam Doubleday Dell
Publishing Group, Inc.

This is a work of fiction. Names, characters, places, and incidents are
used fictitiously. Any resemblance to actual persons, living or dead,
events, or locales is entirely coincidental.

Book design by Chris Welch

Library of Congress Cataloging-in-Publication Data

May, Jesse.
Shut up and deal / by Jesse May. —
p. cm.
I. Title.
PS3563.A9419S58   1998
813'.54—dc21   97-34619
CIP

ISBN: 0-385-48940-4
Copyright © 1998 by Jesse May
All Rights Reserved
Printed in the United States of America

ACKNOWLEDGMENTS

This book is far from a solo effort. It might still remain in a drawer were it not for the Herculean efforts of my editor, Tina Pohlman, who somehow saw through the garbled, grumbled mess that I called a first draft and made it into a novel. Thanks to Heather Schroder, who has guided me from our first meeting over arugula and Parmesan in Frankfurt and whose talents are far too diverse to sum up with the title of literary agent. For help along the way, thanks to Chas Edwards, Spiro, JCBB, Tare, Don Wonderly, Mickey Finn, WC, Mike Danino, Judy and Joanna May, Steve King, Werner Klein, the wonderful staff of the Taj Mahal poker room, and, of course, Sam, Jon, and Luma. My family is my backbone and I'm endlessly grateful to my favorite storytellers, long hours around the dining room table with Paul May, John Slavin, and Bobby Blum. I would always be lost without my wife, Karina, whose constant love and support defy the fact that she married a gambler. And finally, this book is dedicated to the spirit of the unflinchingly honest poker player Cong Do, because he knows what I'm saying.

SHUT UP
AND DEAL

PROLOGUE

IT'S ALL ABOUT cheating. I say cheating and people their faces drop, they get shocked. But it's not the same word I'm thinking about. Because when you're involved in the poker world, the gambling world, you spend every day thinking about that word. And because there aren't many rules, or at least there's a lot of gray areas, really it all just started as shooting angles. And you have to think about it in the context of the history of poker. The history of poker is a history of cheating, and this is not to say that the old poker players were cheaters, but many were hustlers, and they could shoot the angles.

In the sixties and seventies poker was nearly always played No-Limit, or table stakes. In No-Limit poker you can bet anything in front of you all at one time and you only need one good hand to break everyone. In No-Limit it's easier and more likely to bust a mark in one night. Because in the old days there wasn't a casino to walk into every night of the week where the games are arranged for you and the people show up and all the money is guaranteed. No, in the old days games took place all over—houses, barns, skating rinks, hotel rooms—and they went and then they broke. So you had to go in and get the money and leave town and look for the next place. There just wasn't any money in it for the house, no reason for casinos to run a game that just took place for a day or two and thousands of dollars changed hands and then everybody left town and the house didn't get any of it except maybe twelve dollars in rake. It didn't make any sense for them to spread No-Limit poker without cheating too. And a professional gambler had to thrive in that atmosphere. That's the history of poker and when I say there was a lot of shooting angles going on, it just means everybody finds their own ways to get the money.

Then came the late 1980s. A bunch of things happened round about the same time period, or all in a row. The Mirage, California, here come the Indians. And the invention of limit Texas Hold'em poker.

In 1987 there was legalized poker in Nevada and in one county of California. By 1996 poker could be legally played in casinos all over twenty-three states of the Union. And five countries in Europe.

People started playing poker. A lot of people started playing poker and there was *Card Player* magazine and tournaments and books and now instead of ten guys trying to make a living out of the same game at the Golden Nugget, there's ten thousand guys trying to make a living in one thousand poker games in casinos all over the country and at all limits and the money, the money couldn't help but be loose.

Let's make one thing clear. Limit poker was not invented by the poker players. Limit poker is the brainchild of the house and the house is who it's for and the house is who is gonna get the money. Along with a few other people, maybe.

Someone said what if, instead of being able to bet whatever you want at any time, there's a set limit—so people can't win or lose too much per hand. This will make them play longer, and make the games last longer. It also increases the luck factor and lessens the skill. So now if the house is charging players by the hour or taking a nominal amount from each pot, then those nominal amounts are gonna add up. And this is how poker turned into a service industry. All the house has to do is keep people at the table, keep the games going, and their cut is guaranteed. Every pot. Every hour. Chick-chock.

Everybody starts the same way. First you think that there's no possible way to make a living at poker. Then you get involved a little deeper—you run a little lucky, quit your job, start making money and spending high. And then you think that this is the easy life and how sweet it is and the simplest thing in the world is to wake up whenever you want, go into the card room, play a little, and win.

But then you run bad. There's no possible way for you to win—you could be playing head up with a blind man. And then you think that you must be the unluckiest guy in the world and then you go broke and then you borrow some money and then you go really broke and then you decide that there's no possible way to make a living at poker and anyone who says he is is either lying or just has a horseshoe stuck up his ass and hasn't been around long enough to see it turn. Or both.

Everybody wants to know about skill. Who's the best and who's got it and who ain't and what we've got here, and all I can say is that the answer is never that easy. Like for example there's this guy, call him Ace, and he plays well, I mean he plays really well, better than me, like if we were ever to get involved in a heads-up match, Ace would clean me up. And he has. Nothing to it. But one night maybe Ace and I are in a Hold'em game together, and we both have bad luck and we both lose five thousand dollars. Now Ace, what does he do? He gets so mad at losing that five thousand that he stalks off into the pit to try and get even and blow off some steam and he ends up losing twenty thousand more playing craps. Meanwhile, I get so mad at losing my five dimes that I go home, get in my closet, stuff a pillow in my face, and scream until I lose my voice. What's the difference? Twenty thousand dollars. Now who's the better poker player? It ain't that easy.

Or, Ace feels good because he's generally considered the best poker player in the room and in the town, and so when the games are real good and the money is fast and loose, then Ace he won more than a bunch of money. Meanwhile me, the plodder, I'm considered one of the worst and I'm just there showing up every day. After a while the money dries up, lots and lots of people go broke, and the games start getting pretty tough. Sometimes real tough. But Ace, he's still the best Hold'em player in the game, in the room, in the town. So he's still there every day. But now his edge it ain't so big, and now when he wins it ain't so much, and when he runs a little unlucky he's going off big time. Meanwhile, what do I do? When the games start getting tight and the money ain't flowing, I pack up and head off to Austria, where they just opened a new card room and everybody's rich and nine out of ten of 'em are still dumb as a stump. Now does that make me a better poker player? The answer's not so easy.

One more example about Ace. He's a Hold'em player, a Hold'em specialist, Hold'em is his game, and that's all he plays because he don't want to play anything else. And he's just so good at Hold'em, I guess. I'm a Hold'em player too. That's what I started at, that's what I know, and that's where I made my bones. But in Atlantic City in the Taj Mahal something began to happen. Look in the poker room and look who the good players are and nine out of ten of 'em are Hold'em players, that's what they like to play. So all these pros are packing the Hold'em games. Meanwhile, there ain't a fuckin' Stud player in the town and all the live ones, all the marks and the drunks and the guys who are dripping with dead money, when they come into town they're playing Stud. Why? No reason, they just maybe like it better. I start playing Stud. I force myself to learn it, and hell, I may not be that good but I'm gonna play with the idiots. But Ace, he ain't gonna learn no new game. He figures he don't have to because he's so good at Hold'em and he's been playing it for years and years, and for him to get that good at Stud would take so much time it ain't even worth it. He figures. The answer is never so easy. But some people are still here and others have left town in a bus. That's what happens in the poker world. And that's what I mean by shooting angles.

See, poker didn't just start as a hustler's game. I mean it always was and always will be. But what I mean by hustling, well, maybe it's just shooting the angles. Shooting all the angles. Because when you want it bad enough you'll do anything to get the money. People just do what they have to do to survive. To survive. I've seen so many world champions on the rail, and why, because they figure they're so good that there's an angle that they don't have to shoot, something they can let get away. When they're broke they're still the best player, ain't no one gonna argue about that. But there ain't no corporate sponsorships for the top guys. Not yet at least. And when you're down and out, man, who the fuck cares how big your dick is. I mean, I really don't. It's just talk.

Now don't go thinking about who the better poker player is, because I could just as easily tell a hundred stories that make Ace look good and me look like a chump. And what's the moral? What I'm saying is this—there is no reality, it all depends on how I present what is and how I cloud it. And the answer doesn't matter. No, the answer only matters if you're trying to make a judgment, if someone else is making a judgment. It only matters if you got something to prove. But if you're trying to prove something to someone besides yourself, then I say you're in a whole other kind of trouble. That's gonna hurt you too.

In poker, skill ain't a marketable commodity. Skill ain't marketable to no one but yourself. That's it. And that's important.

Poker is a combination of luck and skill. People think mastering the skill part is hard, but they're wrong. The trick to poker is mastering the luck. That's philosophy. Understanding luck is philosophy, and there are some people who aren't ever gonna fade it. That's what sets poker apart. And that's what keeps everyone coming back for more.

ROBBER
BARON

"**S**O I SAY to heem, I hope you die, you motherfucker you." That's what Vinnie the Greek, in his heavy accent, said to Bart Stone a few weeks ago when Vinnie and Bart were both out in Las Vegas for the 1994 World Series of Poker. Most poker players were in Vegas for the series, but not Hot Mama Earl or Jimmy or Mike Luma or me—Vinnie is giving us a recap, heavy on the gossip. The five of us are sitting in an air-conditioned restaurant a few blocks from where Jimmy and I live in Atlantic City, New Jersey. It's about noontime and summer in Atlantic City and outside of the restaurant is sweating hot, especially when you spend all your time in the air-conditioned oxygen-added climate-controlled smoke-filled bright lights shining down and bells ringing and cocktail waitresses prancing around free drinks and very few clothes of the poker room, which is where all of us spend the bulk of our time. Like every waking hour. So we're sitting there and sipping our draft beers, all except for Earl, who's got Perrier, and Mike Luma, who finished his beer in one gulp just because he was hot and thirsty and Mike. I've slipped my sandals off my feet because I'm sitting on a high stool and it's delicious to rest my bare feet on the rungs, silvery metal and cold. Even though I quit smoking again this morning, I'm smoking— we're all smoking from Jimmy's Marlboro Lights—except Hot Mama Earl, who as always is chewing on an unlit cigar. I'm in a good mood because I won this morning and yesterday and I'm going to spend the day in the sun on my patio listening to music and doing the crossword.

I like to listen to Vinnie talk. He's a good guy and funny and I admire him a lot because he's been around poker forever and he's one of the few poker players who my mentor Wayne respects. Vinnie plays really well, mostly tournaments and Pot-Limit, but now he's broke, out of money, and Earl is backing him and Vinnie spends all his time looking for the big score.

Vinnie is originally from Greece and he still speaks with a thick accent. He's broad with a big belly and long curly hair, short thick arms, huge hands, and a lot of gold necklaces and a gold bracelet that says Vince. He knows that I'm intimidated by him at the poker table and have been since I first met him at Foxwoods and thought Vinnie was a living legend because he always plays in the big game and handles himself really cool. And Vinnie dominated everybody in those Foxwoods Pot-Limit Omaha games when he would sit next to Bart Stone and between them they would have all the chips. And I think they were doing business together, like staying out of each other's way and Bart slapping Vinnie's hand one time

when Bart got Uptown Raoul to split the pot with him when
Uptown had two pair and Bart had nothing but a busted wrap
straight draw. But Vinnie and Bart both were backed by Earl
so there must have been something going on. Poker gets kind
of complicated like that, but you can figure that, whatever the
arrangement, Hot Mama Earl was taking the financial worst
of it.

But Vinnie and Bart are different operators and this is two
years later and now Vinnie is broke and sometimes says to me,
"You my fuckin' hero, Mickey," but I think he just says this to
have fun at my strange clothes and the surprising and maybe
inexplicable fact that I been around two years now in the big
games and not gone broke.

Anyway, the past is the past and it gets kind of fuzzy as it
gets old, but Hot Mama Earl and Bart Stone and Hot Mama
Earl's money were together and in late 1993 they drove to Las
Vegas in Earl's Cadillac to take Bart Stone's Seven-Card Stud
game on the road. They lost, or Earl lost, but Earl loved being
with Bart and talking about that drive across the country with
him. "You have no idea, Mick, what a funny man Bart is."
And he tells me about the girl at the drive-thru giving Bart
Stone a hard time, so Bart says in his dry rasp, "I want six
chickens."

Earl really liked Bart, idolized him, and always wanted to
hang with him and watch him play. But now Bart owes Earl
like ninety thousand dollars which Earl was okay with, or I
guess so, until a few months ago when Earl's down in Atlantic
City for a few days, which is what he does. Spends about a
week or so in AC at the poker tables, I swear the guy never
sleeps, and then he goes back up to his home in Hartford for a
while.

This time Earl lost what he brought whether it was in poker or lending money, and rather than get some off his credit card or call home he asks Bart for five hundred dollars to get home. No big deal. Earl was planning on leaving town anyway and he doesn't really take losing too hard, just smiles and says, "Nice hand, Mick," or, "You raised before the flop with that hand, right?"

"Right."

"Just checking, Mick."

Anyway, Earl asks Bart for five hundred dollars just to get home, and in front of the whole poker room Bart says no, he just lost all his money at the craps table, which had to be a lie and a pretty bad one, and I have to think he had the money because everybody did and that night after Earl left town I saw Bart playing in the big game and I guess Earl was about as hot and hurt and embarrassed as he could be. And I guess so, I mean five hundred bucks when you owe the guy ninety thousand and he doesn't press and all you do is hurt the guy in the one place where he can't take it—his pride. Bart embarrasses Earl in front of the whole poker room, his peer group, his friends, or at least that's the way Earl looks at it because he's not there for the money no matter what he says.

Now it's just a few months later and Earl is here saying Bart's the worst cocksucker in the whole world. Vinnie is saying the same thing, but since he's still backed by Earl I think he's mostly talking for Earl's benefit, making Bart look bad so Earl doesn't. I don't really know if Vinnie doesn't like Bart because of Earl or if something happened between them, but it's probably just times change and stuff and it's not like Foxwoods when they played together every day and were the two main men in the big game.

Vinnie is telling us about Bart at the World Series of Poker, and he says, "Bart he go to Vegas and he go broke. Then he borrow some money around or he get some and he go really broke. So now the motherfucker"—here he stops to take a big drink and put his cigarette out emphatically, and he laughs— "the motherfucker he come up to me in the Horseshoe in the middle of the poker room for money or a place to stay he's sleeping in his car the motherfucker he's so broke and I say to heem, I say, 'I hope you die you motherfucker you.' " Now he laughs again and slowly shakes his head. "But he is one crazy motherfucker, that Bart. I tell you, after thees he go out to play golf weeth Yosemite Sam, you know? And Yosemite, he's got Bart in the middle and they beat him for forty thousand. But Bart, he don't pay and now he have to leave town."

Earl leans across and says solemnly, "Guys, I just don't know what Bart is capable of. He is one seriously crazy man. He's insane, Mick!" And I'm laughing and incredulous because I can't imagine somebody who can go around and stiff Earl for ninety thousand dollars and then stiff Yosemite Sam for forty thousand—is it crazy, or ballsy? Isn't someone going to kill him? Aren't they? My eyes are just wide.

I HAVE NOT gone broke. Not since just before I turned twenty-one. Not since my friend Cato staked me seven hundred dollars. Seven hundred dollars that he knew I didn't have. Money to play in a 20-40 game held in the back of an abandoned skating rink just outside of New Orleans, where when we knocked on the door I said, I'm a friend of Buffalo's and I was here one time with Angelo. And the guy who opened the door had a loaded shotgun and there was a pretty girl who cooked us steak while we played. I won twenty-four hundred dollars that night, which was like three months' pay at the Mercy Hospital where I was a paper collator in the records room, and I was off to Las Vegas and northern California and then back to Vegas and then to Foxwoods in Connecticut and then down to Atlantic City with time out for breaks in between, and here I am now playing in the big games in Atlantic City and some scary kinds of shit.

But look, I mean it's always been the same with me. Ever since I started playing poker it seems like it's always been the same. Win a little, lose a little. Stay in action, afford the buy-in, keep my head above water and keep moving, always moving. And watch people go broke. Watch 'em fold up and go broke.

Then I go on a losing streak. Or have one bad night, or whatever. Just something that makes me question everything I know about poker—no, everything I believe—and consider giving up and be scared to go in the card room and not know when to fold or when to raise or when to play or when to stop.

And then it turns around. Pop. Just like that it turns around and I start winning and don't stop winning and start playing higher and faster, and then the cycle starts again. Over the last six years this cycle has been perpetual, and always vicious, and always of lunar-type proportions. And these cycles have been punctuated by leaves of absence, lots of them, because basically I can't deal, I'm dysfunctional, I need to reorient myself, my place in space, my poker philosophy. One time it was two weeks in Jamaica, then two months in Europe, then four months in Israel, then one month across country, later another month across country, then back to Europe. And every time I'm away, I'm away from the table, but the game is right there next to me, it's living with me as I replay hands and people and conversations and games and days and plays and angles. And every time I come back, I break through, my thoughts are different, my understanding feels deeper. And here's the funny part. I always think I understand. And everybody else doesn't. And they're all thinking the same thing.

But the interesting thing about everything I learned about poker is that I never learned it when I learned it, like when a batting coach says, Keep your eye on the ball, and you say, Yeah yeah, I heard all that stuff already, and he says, No, keep your eye on the ball, you know, you hear it but it just sails around like of course, yeah, of course, and then one day I don't know where you'll be, most likely at the poker table but a lot of times you're there even when you're not there, you know waking up sitting on the toilet thinking about a hand and talking to yourself or maybe just the game and what a stupid fuck this one guy is and how he's broke and all of the sudden pow to the front of your brain comes something so simple, so beautifully simply complicated that it makes you want to laugh.

But that's just because poker seems so easy. Anybody can play, anybody can learn. Poker's just a never ending series of hands. During each hand a pot is built and won, money in the center of the green felt-covered table. No beginning and no end, because each hand takes only a minute and then we go on to the next one. You can play one hand or a thousand hands. Five minutes or five days. In limit poker there's usually four betting rounds per hand, fixed bets, and typically the last two bets are double what the first two bets are. So if you're playing in a 10-20 Hold'em game, during the first two betting rounds in every hand all bets and raises are ten dollars, and during the last two rounds all bets and raises are twenty dollars. If the game is 100-200, bets and raises are a hundred and two hundred dollars, and like that.

Poker tables are big, big enough for ten men to sit around plus the dealer, who doesn't play, just runs the game. Seats for up to ten, but Amarillo Slim once told me, it only takes two people to gamble. Yeah, I said. And I ain't one of 'em. He's right, though, the game is the same, two people or ten. It's just that the fewer people you play with, the more often it's your turn to make a decision, and consequently the more often you put money into action. But poker games start and break and swell and shrink and sometimes a game will keep going at the same table for three days or a week. It'll start up with eight and then wane in the wee hours of the night until some new faces come into the room and revive it. So you can be playing for thirty hours and maybe two guys have played right there along with you and everybody else showed up sometime in between and a bunch of guys are waiting to get in the game because they heard some fool is two days in the same seat.

When I say that poker is an easy game to play, I just mean because it is. From the very first time I played poker up until now, the way I play—I mean the basic how to play—is the same. It's the same and it's easy because it's just action that goes round and round the table in a circular fashion and if you're still in the hand after the person on your right acts, then it's your action. And the choices are always the same. If there's no betting yet in the round, then you can check or bet. If someone else has already bet, then you can call, raise, or fold. That never changes about poker and it never has changed and I know it's easy because so often I've seen a guy come in and put a stack of money on the table and be so drunk he can't even hold his cards up and tell everybody at the table, Just tell me how much I owe. And the rules of the casino protect him.

The rules of the casino protect him because the action is always going around in a circle. And when the action comes to you, if you don't know what's going on, if you got your moon face and your big googly eyes on and your head knee deep in a gin and tonic, it just doesn't matter. It doesn't matter because the dealer is still gonna say, It's your action, sir. The dealer is still gonna say, Two-hundred-dollar bet to you, sir, two hundred dollars to play. The game is gonna sit there and the dealer is gonna tell you that you can either pay the money or fold your hand and wait for the next one. And then the action keeps going around again. You don't even have to follow it yourself.

And when the hand's over, if you can't remember the ranking of hands, the fixed hierarchy that all five-card poker hands fall into, it doesn't matter. If you don't know what you got then it's probably time to go home, but never fear because if you flip your hand face up then the dealer is responsible for reading it, the dealer is responsible for reading all exposed hands and determining who won and pushing the pot. So all you have to do is sit there. And that's what I mean when I say that poker is an easy game.

And like a shot I remember one night at the Taj Mahal or was it a day when we were playing 100-200 the three-way game and I had been stuck eleven thousand dollars and I'm a minimum of eighteen hours in the game and we are playing Omaha, high only, which is one step short of madness anyway, short-handed, which is what we are. Me and Jimmy and Kamikaze Will and I don't know who else and one hand the board reads eight-jack-queen and I've got a nine-ten in my hand for the straight and me and Will are raising all the way and a king falls on the river. We both flip over our four cards with nine-ten up front for the straight, splitting the pot. And everybody looks at the hands and sees that it's a split pot. And wouldn't you know Ryan the dealer stares for about two seconds and then darts his hand over the table and fishes an ace out of the back of my hand, showing that I've made an ace-high straight on the river and I win the whole pot. I'm flabbergasted, can't even read my own hand. I want to stand up and hug Ryan, but he's expressionless when I thank him. "Just doing my job," he says. He's already shuffled for the next hand and the cards start zinging. Poker ain't that hard.

THE GAME IS 100-200 Hold'em. I look around the table for the umpteenth time and ask myself how it's possible for me to be stuck in this game. To the tune of eight thousand dollars, no less. It's the Taj Mahal, Atlantic City, where poker's been legal for about a year. The lineup is somewhere between nine monkeys and ten goons. Sitting in the two seat is Vaughn—some guy who just popped in from Canada for a few days.

Nobody knows his deal except that he's full of shit. He's one of those guys who wears a real expensive suit and tries to make everyone think he's real important. Nobody gives a shit, we just want to play cards. Vaughn has got Asian features and he says he's from western Canada, so why the guy has a Deep South type of accent is anybody's guess. It sounds like the kind of voice you use when you're trying to mock someone from the Deep South. Blah, blah, blah, he's just talking and talking, and I'll be honest with you, this guy is bothering the hell out of me. What's worse is he's one of the livest players at the table and I'm scared to death if I open my mouth then he'll leave the table. So I got my trademark shit-eating grin plastered to my face and my teeth are clamped shut to hold the bile down and I've got sunglasses on to hide my eyes and I'm trying to look calm cool and unruffled, not dog tired from already playing for eight hours and not having slept much lately, and losing a lot lately, and just having ducked outside with Russian Alex to smoke a joint out of boredom and frustration so now I'm stoned on top of everything else. But at least I still got the lid on my play and I'm just waiting and watching and shuffling my chips and hoping that I pick up a few good hands sooner rather than later.

Vaughn isn't a newcomer to poker. When he first sits down in the game, despite all the bullshit coming from his mouth like, I'm just a tooooreeest, and You boys are hussslers and whining this and that and Now don't try to raaab me, boys, and stuff, he plays rather tight and doesn't get in the pot unless he has something. That is, until he takes his first bad beat. That's it, one bad hand and the man folds up like a two-dollar suitcase, crumbles like a coffeecake, this man comes unglued. One second he is talking up a storm with his nonstop pitter-patter and calmly lighting his special Dunhill cigarettes from the gold cigarette case with his engraved lighter, folding before the flop with a professional regularity. The next second his eyes are wild, he is smoking like a house, his anxiety is everywhere. He shuffles his chips again and again, faster and faster, and best of all he begins to play every hand and money starts running out of him like water. He also stops talking. Completely.

From my position across the table I see him scared, desperate, and very ready to come off his cheese. I wonder to myself how much he can go off for. He's got about three thousand dollars on the table, but you never know whether or not he's got deep pockets. Now I just pray to pick up a good hand while this clown is shoving money in the pot. This guy Vaughn is like a lot of people who play poker. Most of the time they limit themselves to two options: either they win a little or they lose a lot. Most of this has to do with ego. They want to be able more than anything to say that they beat the game. This is why they're happy to take small wins—hit and run as it may. But guys like Vaughn are completely unable to take a loss. Once they start losing, they rarely leave unless they get even or go broke. Ah, they're wonderful people to have sitting across the table, but you have to get them stuck or else it's good-bye with your money. And as good as a guy like Vaughn plays when he's winning, when he's losing he plays so bad, so fast, and so many hands that the only way for him to win is to get unbelievably lucky all at once. This seems to happen a lot, or maybe it just hurts so much when it happens at my expense that the wounds are slow healing and not oft forgotten. Which is why I feel particularly like getting up, punching Vaughn in the nose, and then breaking his spine over my knee like a piece of kindling. Because while going off like a rocket ship and doing his hotheaded and desperate best to give all his money away, Providence has just delivered him four winning hands in a row, big pots all of them, with hands that make a mockery of order and decorum in a poker game. What do you want from me? Take my word for it the guy had no business being involved in the hands but sometimes you can stick your head in shit and come up smelling like a rose. Not all the time, or maybe it depends on how long you live.

So now he's won like three or four pots in a row and he didn't have to show his last hand and he's really alive now and carrying on, confident because he's getting back in the game. I'm in the small blind and Vaughn raises in middle position just like he has the last four hands and everyone folds to me in the small blind and I've got ace-jack off suit, which I decide is a big hand. I mean the guy can't have anything five consecutive hands, can he? Ace-jack has to have him beat. Or so I think. So I reraise and he reraises and I raise and he just calls. Rags flop, but a jack hits the turn and I bet and he raises and I'm sitting there for a long time to decide if I should raise him back or not, but I just call. And he's looking at me with these big round wide bug eyes. He's not sure and it goes check check on the end and I turn over my ace-jack and he turns over two pocket kings with a relieved smile and takes the pot. And Old Man Sam, who has been watching this hand really closely, turns to me and says, "What are you doing, man? Are you crazy or something?" And at that, man, I just break up laughing.

"Sam, man, I was thinking of reraising that man. I thought I had the best hand for sure. I got top pair, man. I thought it was a big hand!"

"You raise that man five times with ace high. I'm saying you're a damn fool." Old Man Sam always speaks his mind. I look to Jimmy for sympathy, but he's cracking up also. Where the fuck does that guy get pocket kings from? I've gotta get out of here.

But Old Man Sam is a bit mystified by this guy too, because the very next hand he's in there with Vaughn and Johnny World and there's a whole lot of raising going on between Sam and Vaughn, and Johnny World makes a last-card flush but everyone calls on the end. And when Vaughn throws his hand in, conceding defeat, Old Man Sam is perched way up in his chair on his knees picking at his two cards and he says, "Wait a damn minute. I want to see that man's hand. I got a right to see it, don't I? I mean, I want to see what cards that damn fool was playing with. I mean look here, I had a pair of damn aces, man, I want to know what that man was raising back and forth with like that. That man was raising me!" And we are all in hysterics, because Old Man Sam he just tells it like it is. What the hell was that guy Vaughn doing anyway, six damn hands in a row?

This guy will go off his cheese and be broke at some time, but it's not tonight, not anymore, and I know this for sure because I can see the signs of the man who knows he escaped death and is now looking for the quick exit. He sits back in his chair for the first time in maybe an hour, takes a deep breath, looks down at how many cigarettes he just smoked, is surprised, and his eyes come back into focus and begin to lose that glazed look, he gets happy, and now he starts talking. I mean talking. Because he got even and now he's ahead and he's the big man again.

But I'm not looking at him right now. I'm looking at the

guy sitting next to him, who he beat a few pots ago and who's one of the other players stuck big in the game. I'm staring at Jimmy. And Jimmy's staring at me, and even though we both have dark sunglasses on and cool-rider mask face freezes we're both looking at each other and thinking the same thought across that long green table. Well, here we are again. And in a way it's funny and when we're both home and dog tired in about fifteen hours we'll sit on the couch and laugh. We'll laugh because we don't want to cry. But we also know that if it wasn't for nights like this there wouldn't be nights like that. What I mean is that that's why there is so much money in poker, why so many people play it for money, and badly. In chess or pool, it's impossible to get lucky. The best player always wins unless he dogs it, which is where hustlers come from. In poker, even the absolutely worst players can get lucky and win sometimes. Sometimes a lot. But that's what keeps them coming back and coming back. That, and a lot of people think it's a hell of a lot of fun.

But no one enjoys losing. Jimmy and I are just better at it than most people. I don't think Vince Lombardi would like us. He said a good loser is a loser. Jimmy and I are just sitting there and waiting for our turns. We hope.

One saving grace is that, even should Vaughn leave, this game is still rocking. I mean, he isn't the only one this game is built around, just the guy who happens to be playing the worst at the moment. And to be honest for a minute, he's the guy I would most like to beat. That is if I let my feelings get involved, but they only can go so far. You've got to make decisions based on money and not how you feel about a guy, so if my uncle Chester was playing and he was bad, I'd either have to play him hard or not play. You know, one thing you can't control is when you'll get a good hand and you either have to make the most of it or it's just another leak with the power to drive you broke.

Russian Alex is sitting in the one seat, next to the dealer, and he doesn't play Hold'em any too well. He's an excellent Stud player, I mean really good, and a pretty dominant guy in the poker room. And he likes me, because I'm half Russian or because I lent him a thousand dollars no problems no questions and didn't say When are you gonna pay me back, just Pay me when you can. He was down, way down, we're talking broke, and me who never lends money did it, why, because I like him and I trust him, and also because he knows everybody in the room and he's a strong personality and a good guy to have on your side and now he says in his thick Russian accent, "Anybody want to fock weeth Mickey they fock weeth me!" He paid me the money right back a few days later because he ran good with it and then I lent him again the next week, but I only gave him four hundred dollars this time.

Now I always tell him that I'm losing so maybe he thinks I'm on my way broke too, or more likely he just thinks I'm rich because every time he sees me he says, Mickey, how you doing, and I say, No good. So he thinks I lose most of the time, which is the same as everyone else in the room, because I play it very close to the chest. And once you're not so worried about your ego it's much better to have people think that you lose all the time, because then they think that you're a live one and they don't ask to borrow so often. But anyway, Russian Alex is in the game because there's no big Stud game tonight and he's been doing well this week so he's a little pumped, but Hold'em's not his game and he's a little bit on tilt, so he's good for the game right now.

Sitting next to him is Vaughn, who looks like he's leaving any second, and then Jimmy, who plays as good as anyone or better and almost never cracks. So I'd prefer if he went home, but he's my number one buddy and my roommate and I'd rather see him do well than anyone except me, of course. Next to Jimmy there's two other guys who are semilive, that is they play pretty often but they have jobs and they don't play well they just like the action, and then there's Old Man Sam. He can't play a lick and he knows it, but he's so rich he don't really care. He's retired and just likes to be here because he likes the action and knows all the guys and doesn't really care about the money, just his ego.

Then there's Johnny World, who's sitting next to me and is one of the ten best pool players in the country, but he's twenty-four and burnt out already. He's sick of pool and can't get anyone to play him anymore and now he plays poker, which he's a champion at already. He's just got so much talent but no discipline and even though he may be the best player in the room, he can't manage a bankroll and he can't hold on to money so he's got his case money on the table right now and even though he can borrow in about a hundred places he's playing careful with it—real careful—maybe too careful, and he's not running real lucky anyway. And so now he's wounded and hurt and every time he loses a hand he kind of shakes his head slowly in disbelief and mumbles to himself, "This is sick."

So right now he's not much of a threat in the game and he's got a lot of other things on his mind like is he gonna go broke and where's he gonna raise some money. He's not really concentrating but just sitting there in a fog and watching the game go round and his money drip away. On the other side of me is DB, one of the Baltimore boys and a super nice guy who owns a furniture store and has got a wife and a six-year-old son who he loves to take to see the Orioles. But since this poker room opened up a year ago he's spent a lot of time in the Taj Mahal and I would have to say that the majority of people who spend their time in poker rooms don't have much of a family life. But DB is a real mellow guy and he doesn't bitch or moan like a lot of other guys when he loses a hand, just says, Nice hand, Mick, in kind of a calm voice and doesn't throw his cards at the dealer or the muck, just kind of checks them over once more and then lays them face down with a tired sigh where the dealer can get them and then stares off into space and waits for the next hand. He plays good and tight and aggressive but he's been running real bad lately and just can't seem to make a win no matter what he does. So he's playing short stacked and he's looking pretty hurt right now and it looks like he keeps making up his mind to leave and then stay and he doesn't really have a stack of chips, just four orange thousand-dollar chips. Which is plenty of money, it's just that everybody knows he didn't win it in no pot or poker game because orange chips only come from the pit like when you play craps or when you borrow some money off a friend who's running hot at blackjack and it's not Can I borrow a few thousand but more like Hey, how about letting me have a few of those orange chips that you got spare sitting on the black- jack table next to a shot of Sambuca. And then he really doesn't know what to do, he just wants to win but maybe is in one of those funks where you just feel like you don't know how. And maybe he's thinking he should really be home and not in the poker room or is his wife going to be mad at him or whatever. He's just got troubles on his mind and not poker.

So all in all it's a pretty good game. It's a very good game and the pots are big, but the live ones have all the money and they might leave. I just wish I could pick up a hand soon because this game doesn't have a lot of staying promise. I mean two guys already left with big loads and all the wrong guys are stuck. And if the three live guys with all the chips take off as they maybe are wont to do, the game will break up in ten minutes flat and I'll be left with no option but to put what's left of my money and chips in my box, go up the escalator, trudge to the parking lot, climb in my car, and when I'm sure that no one can hear me, yell "Aarghh" at the top of my lungs before driving home and collapsing into a fitful sleep plagued by poker nightmares of cards, chips, and disreputable characters robbing and cheating me ad infinitum.

So there we are, sitting at a big green poker table in the high-limit section of the Taj Mahal, which is in the back, away from everything else, and is brightly lit from overhead in the no-time casino style so you never know what time it is. And it's cold because they turn the temperature way down in the middle of the night so people don't get sleepy and they pump more oxygen into the air for the same reason and the only guys who look like they might be sleepy are Vaughn and the other two big winners, but they're probably looking for an excuse to quit the game anyway. And I'm not feeling sleepy at all—just tired—and believe me there's a difference, because you never feel sleepy when you're losing and you never have nightmares when you're just sleepy.

So being that it's the biggest game being played right now

in the poker room and in the whole town for that matter, and being that the table is covered with piles of green and black chips and hundred-dollar bills and is a pretty humming-type game with a lot of bets and raises and big pots and last cards, the customary little crowd gathers to watch, craning their necks. It's some guys playing in the smaller games who just want to railbird for gossip's sake or brokes who are hoping to borrow some money or think maybe someone will just toss 'em a red bird or a black bird. Or they've got even bigger dreams, but those are mostly dreams.

But sometimes if you can catch a guy right after a big win then he's an easier touch and he'll still hem and haw, but a broke might be able to squeeze a few hundred out of him that will rarely to never get paid back. Some people think that it's kind of a winner's tax that they pay and spread the money around a little bit and then when they run bad or go broke everybody will help them out a little too. But maybe they're thinking that they have a peer group and they have some buddies in there and they haven't found out that everybody hates you under their breath if you're doing well, that poker peers feel no sympathy and no pity for you when you're doing bad, they're merely glad it's not them and move in for the kill like big buzzards who know it's much easier taking money from someone on his way down. Some people just can't say no.

And so there's always one to five guys just railbirding the game. But when you're playing, no one likes having some guy you don't know watching, craning his neck to see your cards, silently counting the money in front of you and maybe planning to borrow or rob you or jump you or just find out your business and tell it to everyone else. And that's why they often have a security guard to watch the big game or a floorman to come over and tell the rail not to stand too close, or that if they're not a friend of someone who's playing they have to move on, which is nice because I really don't like to have to do it myself. I don't want to cause bad blood or give the impression of being high and mighty, and I haven't forgotten that it's not so long ago when I was on the rail myself. No, I like to be able to devote myself entirely to the game and watch the hands and watch the players and have everything else done for me. Like the dealer who keeps the game moving, always moving, and who takes care of all the cards and shuffles and says, Your action, sir, or, Raise, or reads the hands at the end and awards the pots and rakes the chips in. And if it's a good dealer like Ryan or Paul then he solves any problem that comes up and keeps the players happy by being alert and knowing the rule or calling the floorman over to solve the big problems and the waitresses who bring drinks and cigarettes or aspirin.

I turn around and there's a young guy standing a few feet behind me, watching the game. He looks familiar but I can't place him, so I ignore him. I mean the poker world isn't so big a place, and when you've played in Las Vegas and California and New Orleans, Chicago and Michigan and Connecticut, Amsterdam and New York City, you see familiar faces all the time, guys you see every day and then not for three years. But that doesn't make them a friend. And the longer you've been around the poker world the more nonplused you get about seeing a familiar face, and while you smile at the front of your mouth the alarm in the back of your head is buzzing and it's saying, What does this guy want from me. And after you've been around and hung with a guy and then not seen him, when you sit down at a table a few years later and there he is

in the three seat you just say, Hey, what's up and how's the
weather in California and I hear the action's good out there.
But I don't say anything that means anything and it's no big
deal because one person's just like another in the poker world.
People drift in and out so fast as they move around, go broke,
quit poker, then come back to poker. Or maybe they just don't
play as often in card rooms anymore, sticking to smaller home
games and just going to Las Vegas for an annual pilgrimage.
And so there aren't really hellos and good-byes so much as
fade in and fade out, and it's amazing how once you start
playing in the big game everyone knows your name and
wants to talk to you and say, How's it going, Mick, and hear
who's winning or losing in the big game and all eyes following me when I walk in or across the room. Or maybe it's just
the crazy ass clothes I'm wearing. But after a while I feel like
as far as new friends go, I'm just not hiring and come back
again later.

So there's maybe four or five guys watching the game and
since I'm sitting on the side of the table people pass if they're
walking by the game, these guys are all standing behind me,
which I don't really like, me being naturally suspicious and
feeling like some guy will reach over my shoulder and grab
one of the rubber-banded packets of hundreds sitting on the
table in front of me and take off down Atlantic Avenue, as
Old Man Sam likes to say. So now I have to watch them and
my money, and they're crowding closer and closer when
there's a big pot. They want to watch the action and see the
hands, so they're bending their heads and necks in and around
to get a glimpse of my cards as I look at them, but I don't like
guys seeing my cards so I keep them real low. Like what if
one of them has got a friend at the table to give signals to?

This is unlikely—mostly they're just curious—but I still don't like people back there close behind me. It disturbs my concentration and I don't want to give anyone an extra line on my play, I don't care who they are, and so I wish the floorman would come over and tell these guys to move on. But he's disappeared for a while, probably because it's late at night and the room's not so busy now. Cleaning people are vacuuming the floor and emptying ashtrays and making everything look spiffy, so it's a good time for the floorman to duck out for a cigarette break and leave these railbirds crowding our game a little too close for my comfort.

This guy's right behind me now and since it's between hands and nothing's happening except for the dealer shuffling the cards and moving the button and saying, "Blinds please," I turn around to look and the guy says, "Remember me?" And now I do remember him from some years ago in Las Vegas when I'm playing 10-20 at the Mirage and Luma's met this guy our age, which is rare in Las Vegas. The guy's working at the Mirage for the summer as a groundskeeper and playing poker on the side, and I sit next to him one night for a few hours in a 10-20 Hold'em game while I am getting hammered and he hit and runs for a nice score. So I guess I do know the guy, but definitely not his name as I only met him once before. But he comes on like we're long-lost friends and it's easy to tell he's not a player, by which I mean he doesn't spend all his time in public card rooms, so he's caught up in all the glamour and mystery of the big game. And so he starts talking loud about how he knew me when I was still playing 3-6 and 10-20 at the Stardust and not one and two hundred, which is the last thing I want some guy to talk about at a table when I'm trying to come on like a major live one by the way I dress and not let on that I'm here to win. And certainly not try to spread it around about how long I've been playing poker and just shit that it ain't no place for your image to talk about at the table, stuff that might make a guy reconsider playing three-handed with me. Like maybe later in the night when the game is looking to break and maybe there's just me and two live ones who don't want to quit because they're stuck, but they also don't particularly like playing short-handed and especially not with a pro, which is how the groundskeeper is telling it. But when they look over and I'm wearing yellow pants and a green double-breasted jacket from the seventies and a green and yellow flowered shirt with dark sunglasses and hair halfway down my back, I really don't look very dangerous.

So now this guy's taken my acknowledgment as an excuse to get real close and he says, "How much are those purple chips worth," pointing to one on the bottom of my stack. And I say five hundred dollars in a low voice and he whistles and keeps on with this and that and shit about poker and I say to him, "Look, it's nice to see you and I'd be happy to talk to you when I'm not playing, so maybe if you'll be around tomorrow." And he says, "Nope, I'm just here tonight," and completely fails to take the hint and continues on in his poker-student-of-the-game manner, which is not a mode I care to be in at the moment, and I just wish the guy would go away and leave me and my no sleep and stuck eight thousand dollars and let me use my remaining energy to try and make some order in the world and be on top of the rhythm of the game.

But no, he keeps on and I'm getting a little sullen and when he says to me in a voice that the entire table can't help but hear, "I'd just like to know one thing—in your opinion what is the biggest difference between playing 100-200 and 10-20?" I look at him and say, "The limit—this is a different limit," and he gives me an uncomprehending look and then smiles because he thinks I'm joking and says again, "No, really, I mean what's the major difference in play in these games?"

And I say, "The chips are different values—these chips are worth more money." And I say it completely deadpan and now he thinks I'm taking the piss out of him and he wipes the smile off his face and his body tenses up and he's a big guy with a weight-lifter-type body. I see Johnny World is trying hard not to laugh and keeping his eyes down and I really wish this guy would leave and I say, "You see if we were playing 10-20 we would be using red chips, but we're not."

And everybody thinks I'm trying to make a fool out of this guy and maybe he suddenly feels like a fool, but I'm just saying the only completely honest thing that I can. But it's not what this guy wants to hear, and I know what he wants to hear, being that he's some guy who spent a summer in Las Vegas and got caught up in poker and gambling and maybe ran good for a little while but not too good. Because when the summer was over he went back to his college and his fraternity where he drinks with his buddies and talks real importantly like he knows secrets about poker and gambling since he's read Larry Sandtrap and heard about Phil Helmuth and seen Johnny Moss and read the careful and analytical articles from *Card Player* magazine where edified players in residence discuss the most technical and elusive aspects of Hold'em, like the different merits of an ace-king and ace-queen in a triple-raised pot. And he wants me to come on like that and give him some line like, Once you fully understand the standard deviation as it regards the higher-limit games and especially the decreasing value of extra bets with suited cards, you will be able to outthink other world champions who continue to semibluff. Or some shit like that, but that's all it is. Shit.

Like when Jamie the lawyer has been playing poker every night he can in private games in New York and at the Mayfair Club and on weekends coming down to Atlantic City and getting a room at the Taj but never using it for sleeping because he plays for forty-eight hours straight—he just loves the action, can't get enough of it, and he loves the players and the mystery and the romance and he entertains some notions of being the best Hold'em player. He does in fact play well—really well—but there's a big difference between playing good poker and getting the money, and what Jamie really wants is fame, not money. He wants to walk in the room and have everyone say, There goes Jamie, the best Hold'em player in Atlantic City and maybe the country, and have his picture in *Card Player* magazine or on the cover when he wins the World Series of Poker and is crowned world champion of poker for the year—la de dah. So Jamie's playing poker all the time he can but he's still got this lawyer job, which I have to assume he doesn't like or at least not as much as poker. And when you play poker all the time and you win for a little while you think, Why not make poker my job and then I'll be doing what I want to do and get paid for it, and you see other people who are doing it and they sure don't play any better than you or at least don't appear to. So Jamie is thinking about taking six months off from work to move down to Atlantic City and play cards full time, and he's talking to anyone who will listen and taking advice from everybody who has an opinion about if he's good enough and can he beat the big game, and how much he's won of this and that in so-and-so time and hourly win rates and so on. And one day he looks me up because someone told him that maybe I was respected or could help him with this or that, so he comes over to me from where he's playing 20-40 one night when I'm in the big game and asks if I mind talking to him when I'm not playing. And I say sure, no problem, even though I've got no kind of information that he wants to hear because I'm a cynic and not a romantic and because he's already got his mind made up about what's important and what's not—he just wants confirmation. So after I'm finished playing one night Jamie and I go over to an empty corner of the room and take two seats at an empty poker table and Jamie lights up a Marlboro Red and I say, "Can I bum a cigarette?" and light one up myself and take a deep drag and feel ten hours of play over my body and I'm tired and cynical and sour.

Now he's telling me that he's making the jump and what can I tell him about his play or the game or the big game and so on and is he good enough. And I say, "Jamie, all I can tell you is that it's lonely out there, real fuckin' lonely, and your play doesn't matter so much as how tough you are and whether or not you fall apart."

Jamie smiles knowingly at this because I'm giving him no new information. But it's possible to be staring straight at something and see right through it, or hear something but stay deaf to its meaning, or be so caught up in the wonderfulness of playing poker and running good and winning money and bullshitting with the guys and finding funny and different ways to say raise and stack your chips and go for massage and eat for free at the Chinese restaurant with a comp some guy you play with received for a little craps action, and watch-

ing the big game and how much Bart won or lost or bet on
football, and how this guy played the deuce-seven or called on
the end or made a 50-1 shot, and whether the cute waitress
will be at Los Amigos bar when she gets off her shift and if it
should be a Coke with or without ice.

And so Jamie quits his job and takes up residence in the Taj
Mahal poker room and begins to play in the big game every
day and do pretty well and make some wins and some money.
And now he's got his confidence together and wants to play
everyone head up to prove he's the best and cool and he's the
man in the poker room and always has a story or a joke for his
eager poker groupies. And now he's got more money laying
around in the box and his pockets and he lends a little here
and there to some buddies and life is real sweet and there's no
one he won't play, no game too tough, until one day I walk
into the Taj and he's sitting there playing with Crazy Roger
and Virginia, who can't really be considered live ones except
for Roger in special circumstances like when he's real stuck or
drinking or coked up or something. But Jamie's the one who's
on tilt, who looks tired now. Jamie in the same seat for
twenty-two hours and having lost five plays in a row at
100-200 or higher, so he's off like sixty thousand inside a
week, which he never thought could or is supposed to happen.
But it does and he did and I don't know how much he's got
but that it hurts him bad. I mean no matter what you got you
don't leave more than that lying around unattached, and just
a few months ago he was playing 15-30 and maybe 30-60.
And when I look at him now with his three-day whiskers and
uncombed black hair, hunched over in his seat smoking cigarette after cigarette with a piddly small pile of chips in front
of him as Crazy Roger and Virginia tread the waters around

him and move in for the kill, and when I hear Roger offering
to lend him some money when he goes all in so he can keep
playing with them (Crazy Roger and Virginia aren't stupid,
they know when fruit is ripe for the picking), all I can think is
the same thing over and over in my head: it's lonely out there.

And all of Jamie's poker friends, all his buddies with their
jokes and games and How ya running and Can you spot me a
thousand and You're the best player in the room, Jamie, and
this and that, who were all by his side when he was way up,
where are they all now? They're all in the corner, whispering,
pointing, and smiling among themselves that secret smile
they save for someone who gets what's coming to them. Or
they're waiting to get in the game.

But back to the groundskeeper. I give it to the guy straight
the only way I know how. But he doesn't want to hear it. He
wants me to be Wild Bill Hickok or Bobby Fisher. But I'm
not, I'm just another sod with dirty hands. I want to turn
around and grab the guy. I want to shake him. I want to
shout, "Look at me! Listen to me! There is no difference in
play!" But I don't say any of that. I just repeat in a small
voice, "This is a higher limit. The game is exactly the same as
10-20 but we use different chips."

Now the kid's mad. I think he wants to hit me. He comes
over all fawning like we were best friends when I was a little
man and now I shouldn't forget where I came from now that
I'm big man. But that's all his way of looking at it. I was just a
guy then and I'm just a guy now, but if I was sitting and
playing 10-20 it would not be the same to this guy—no, he
would have passed me right by.

So now he's pissed. He's decided I'm not so friendly and
acting high and mighty and not giving him an answer to his

question even though I did. I've got my back to the guy and I just wish he would go away. I'm not sure if I can or want to handle this when John the floorman appears like manna from heaven, taps the guy on the shoulder, and tells him he can't stand that close to the game. Saved. The guy vanishes after giving me one last, meet me again and you're dead, hotshot, look. DB sits back down next to me. I hadn't noticed he was gone.

"I thought you looked like you needed a little help," he says, tilting his head toward the floorman. Good old DB. If you ever need anything, all you have to do is ask, DB baby.

Johnny World says, "It would have been funny if it wasn't so obvious you were fucking with him."

"But, John," I say, "I wasn't fucking with him, I was being dead serious."

Johnny World is a smart guy, but he thinks I'm crazy. Or maybe just strange. He says, "Yeah, right." Lights a cigarette, and goes back to the game. So do I.

I DON'T KNOW where the beginning is. But I always come back to what I'm wearing at the time. Those kooky clothes are more real to me than anything else in the poker world. And I know people think I'm strange. But special clothes always go together with poker. At least in my world.

In high school we'd have games every weekend either at Bob's house or in Sal's back room or on my third floor. And I

always brought my bag of poker props. While they were dol-
ing out chips I'd change into my lucky Yankee boxer shorts,
withered to shreds, which were only used for poker until April
'87 when I pledged not to take them off until the Yankees
lost their first game and they went 8 and 0. Pretty smelly. I'd
put on my Budweiser cap, my Team Giants T-shirt, and my
mustard-yellow Velcro-flap Italian sneakers. And when I put
my lucky Moses statue on the table in front of me to ward off
the bad spirits, the guys would deem me fully ridiculous. But I
wouldn't call it superstition. I'd call it getting in the mode.

Seems like things happen too fast to think about the past.
Or remember the beginning. But of course I still remember
the first time I went broke at the poker table. Spring of '87,
my dad was going to Vegas and my friend Matt and I convinced him to take us along. He agreed to bring us to Vegas,
but I'm sure he never expected us to get into the casinos. Matt
looked like he was about twelve, and I guess I didn't look
much older. But I sprouted a small beard and decided to take
dressing seriously.

I'm sixteen years old and when I walk into the poker room
of the Las Vegas Hilton sporting a three-week scruff and
wearing a blue and white striped poplin summer suit, a straw
hat, dark glasses, and duck shoes, nobody even questions me
twice about my age. But I sure get some funny looks. Good to
look weird. The way Matt says it, the last thing I look like is
some kid trying to look older. I look more like a fifty-five-
year-old recluse madman, and in a place like Vegas, hey, that's
okay.

I'm still convinced Matt brought me down. At the
Landmark casino we're playing in a Stud game, one- to four-
dollar limit, and after Matt wins a pot the lady who he beat

stands up and says in a loud voice, "Son, I've got food in my refrigerator that's older than you." The entire table breaks up laughing and the floorman has no choice but to ask us for ID.

But who cares. I mean we were young and Vegas was wild and wonderful. We got thrown out of more than a few joints, but this was the old days and the strip was just filled with casinos and we managed to gamble at quite a few of them before getting carded. Casinos upon casinos, along with a real Vegas show replete with jugglers and rows of bare-breasted women wearing plumage and kicking their legs. And dinner at Caesars Palace on their Japanese barge. Our eyes were wide.

Poker was just another game then. I mean we had craps systems to think about, blackjack and roulette and all types of gambling besides poker. But we did learn the rules to Texas Hold'em, we called it Puggy after our hero Puggy Pearson, poker champion of the world. It was a relatively new game back then before the Mirage opened, before California exploded.

We found a magazine advertising the World Series of Poker 1987 to be held at Binion's Horseshoe casino. Blue and yellow and glossy and filled with pictures of professional poker players who'd competed in previous series. That magazine got more dog-eared than a kid's first *Playboy* when Matt and I brought it back to New Jersey. Our poker crew took it to heart, fighting over who could read it at the table, who got to be who, and who was the meanest toughest ramblin' gamblin' man around, as we dreamed about guys so cool they could make a living at poker and have names like The Cigar and The Oriental Express and Suds and Spats and Slim and man.

But back to going broke. I'd been trying to get in action the whole weekend we were there, but because of Matt and my father and dinners and whatever, I never managed to gamble for more than an hour at a time and so it's our last night and I've still got five hundred bucks cash out of the six hundred that I brought. This would not do, I thought, staring at the ceiling at midnight knowing that we have a ten o'clock flight and I've got a big urge to gamble. Blood pumping, adrenaline flowing, you know the score. I jump out of bed, put on my poplin suit, and descend to the nether world. A night prowler.

All I remember about that night is the hat and the robber baron. I walk into the poker room, sucker painted across my forehead, and don't you know I get talked into playing three-handed Stud, five- and ten-dollar, which at the time is big limit, biggest I ever played by far. It was me and an old local retiree and a hat. First hat I ever played with. A hat is a guy from Texas who smokes a big cigar and wears a real cowboy hat and dresses fine and knows how to gamble. One hand I bluffed 'em both for about a dollar-fifty and the hat says to me, "So, you're a regular robber baron, aren't you?" Which made me feel proud and feel like I wanted to bluff more often, and I guess they cleaned me out in no more than an hour and a half. Five hundred and twenty-five bucks. Lotta money for a sixteen-year-old kid. My first time going broke. First time going upstairs to the room and having one of those fitful sleeps plagued with poker hallucinations and stomach churnings and no, I didn't tell my dad, that's for sure. Just wanted real bad to come back.

I guess I went to Vegas about fifteen times before I turned twenty-one. I went broke about fourteen of those times. Borrowing money, calling home, false deposits in the ATM machine, maxing out credit cards, taking my coin collection to the pawnshop, taking my Walkman and binoculars to the pawnshop, collecting a dollar souvenir chip from every casino at the beginning of my trip and then going back to the casinos at the end of my trip to trade in the dollar chips to get enough money to take a cab to the airport. And then gambling that money away anyhow. If you can figure out how to beat Vegas, then I guess you can damn near do anything.

Like me and Sal, who jetted in while creating a long weekend from college. Day one was just beautiful, one of those times when everything clicks and you look around and smile broadly and think how smart you are to be missing Calculus 151, sitting in a 3-6 Hold'em game sipping the Hilton's famous chocolate milkshake and laughing at Fat Marvin the dealer, who's killing time off shift by drinking it up in the eight seat.

But don't worry, Sal and I both ended up broke. When we walk out of the Las Vegas Hilton poker room to catch a shuttle to the airport, we have forty-seven dollars between us. "Hold it," says Sal as we pass a craps table on the way to the exit. "I just want to make this appropriate." He puts the forty-seven bucks on the pass line and sevens out. Man, there's nothing more sickly than those plane rides home from Vegas.

I'M TWENTY-ONE YEARS old, and as I walk into the Mirage I feel like a big man. I'm wearing my purple and black nylon jogging suit and dark sunglasses and I got Bob Dylan

going on the Walkman as I come in the side door and head
straight for the poker room. Two A.M. and I just woke up and
my hair's still wet and with my blinders on I'm oblivious to
the bells and lights and cheers of the craps and the blackjack
and the slots that I have to bypass to get to the steadily
pulsating card room, like a heartbeat in the middle of the
casino.

It's no time before I'm in a cooking 10-20 Hold'em game.
Saucy kid. Young, brash, and I pull out a big roll of bills and
buy in for five hundred, a whole rack of red chips. I look
around the table. Four familiar faces, five strangers, and me.
I'm focused and my music is loud and good and I don't have
to talk to anyone. Bear down and lock on. I know how to play
this game. Lots of chips on this table, big pots, and people are
playing all kinds of cards and I'm bouncing around to the beat
as I fold my cards. Sometimes I turn off the Walkman when
I'm in a big pot, listen to what I can't watch.

I live in Vegas now, been here three months. It's almost
two years since I dropped out of college. I had classes on
Tuesday and Thursday mornings, and our poker games were
Monday and Wednesday nights. Irreconcilable differences.
Now I live in an apartment two blocks from the Mirage and I
have a poker-player roommate and a car and a good 10-20
bankroll and I'm focused and playing lots of short sessions.
Hit and run at three in the morning, and I'm scouting the
games from the Mirage to the Stardust to the Horseshoe at all
hours. Poker, poker, poker, I'm like Larry Sandtrap, coldly
analyzing each flop and each situation and trying to win one
and a half bets per hour.

I'm a professional, I think. I live here and I look like a
poker professional and I been on a good winning streak lately

and I'm just loving the hell out of it. And the live ones come in and I outplay 'em and I'm gonna take the money. Finally, finally I'm a professional poker player, just like I wanted to be, finally I'm here in the Mirage at one in the morning with a pocketful of money and a game I'm getting proud of. Too proud.

Big red-faced guy sitting in the one seat, drunk and drinking, talking loud. Fiftyish, beefy red face, needles, likes to needle. He's on a bit of a rush, two big pots, and big speeches after both hands and I've got my Walkman off now because I just got beat in one of those pots and I'm a little bit hot and going over the hand to see if I'm happy how I played it. And this guy's talking it up.

Red Face wins another pot, he's chirping now. He beats an old man sitting in the eight seat, maybe sixty-five or seventy, a tourist and not at all comfortable in the game and doesn't know very much about Hold'em and it's true, yeah, old man plays terrible, but he's pleasant and quiet and is just sitting there playing his cards with his own money.

I mean look, this old guy is maybe first or second time playing Hold'em. He's got less than a clue, but I guess he's been lucky all day, real lucky, and he's ahead in the game when I sit down. But he ain't saying nothing or being a jerk, just an old retired guy in town with his wife for some fun and here he is at this poker table while his wife is playing the slots but he likes it because he's running lucky and so he sends his wife back to the hotel or wherever and stays on playing into the night at the Mirage in the poker room when the owls come out and the sharks are feeding, but luck's made to be pressed a little.

Because the old man is in every pot and Beefy Face starts winning almost every pot, the old man is certainly taking the worst of the beating. But that's not all, because Beefy Face isn't content to win the money alone. Swaying slightly in his seat, he wants to win the gut money, too, and every hand is accompanied by a diatribe. But that's not all, because he has to get personal, too.

"I don't know what you're doing in that pot, fella, you're really stupid, you ain't even got a pair. Where'd you learn how to play? Excitement too much for you over there, old man? How old are you, anyway? Too old to be playing Hold'em. . . . Look like you're gonna die in your seat over there. . . . Haw haw haw. . . . Nearing the end, huh partner? Haw haw haw. . . ."

Wow, what an asshole, and he's really running lucky. Jerkoff, I sure hate guys like this, gotta make some poor fella feel bad, livest guy at the table.

About forty minutes later, Beefy must be ahead fifteen hundred dollars. He's got so many chips he can't even rack them. Just keeps playing and talking and insulting and picking away at the old man, and no one at the table is saying anything. Old man don't play enough poker, feels too strange here to defend himself, and no one at the table is saying anything because hell, it's a poker game and it's late at night and we all just want to get even or win some money and words and emotions are supposed to roll over players like waves on the ocean. But I'm hot, I'm hot because I'm losing and I'm hot because I got my Walkman turned off now and my sunglasses focused on a big red face and a gin and tonic and most of the red chips on the table and finally he loses a pot, wouldn't you know it, a last-card draw-out by the gray-haired old man—two outer. Old man makes trips on the end and doesn't even bet it, just checks and calls and now Beefy Face's mouth opens up big and ugly.

"You stupid ass, what do you think I got, Rip Van Winkle, you're throwing your money away. What is this, your last night on earth? You taking your last breath over there, dumb ass?" And on and on and the poor old guy just kind of sits there feeling real bad and raking his pot and when Beefy Face takes a break to sip his gin and tonic I can't hold back.

I sit up straight in my chair and look right at him and say, "Hey . . . uh, you know you're not looking too healthy your-self, OLD MAN!" Say it with a bite, punk kid wearing a new jogging suit and sunglasses and all cocky and hotshot and he looks at me and looks at me and his features are all twisted up and eioughhh. With hate in his eyes and he just doesn't say anything. I'm kind of shaking a little bit and I probably shouldn't have opened up my big mouth, but I got that table there between us.

And I'm the man, I'm the man in this town and I'm a professional and come pick on me, tough guy, I got your game, I got it, man. Yeah.

Miraculous thing happens just after that. Beefy Face starts losing, every hand. Some bad luck and some fast play and some bad hands and his chips start to shrink and I win a monster pot with a king-jack when I make a straight on the turn, and all of the sudden I'm ahead in the game and it's rocking and Beefy is losing 'em as fast as he won them and a new dealer comes in and a half hour passes and I turn my Walkman back on and start bouncing to the music again and stare straight at Beefy Face with my mirrored sunglasses, and

watch this man who's now on tilt and not hitting any cards to
boot and someone's pulled the drain plug on his chips and he's
given back maybe nine hundred or so in an hour, big numbers
in 10-20. I've already drunk three coffees and a cranberry
juice and I can't hold it so when the big blind comes to me I
get up and hustle for the bathroom, don't want to miss too
many hands.

Mirage bathroom, right next to the poker room, most beautiful public bathroom in Vegas, maybe in the world. Big rows
of white sinks and mirrors in the front room and I walk
through, through the acre of urinals to the stalls at the back,
which they clean almost every time someone goes in so there's
always a bright new one just been wiped and incensed and
powdered, and I pee and I pad back out past the stalls, past
the urinals, and I'm thinking, Okay, you're doing good, play
tight. I'm passing the rows of mirrors and I look up and
there's Beefy Face right in my face with a kill look and he
grabs me by my zippered jacket front and almost lifts me off
the ground. And as he pushes me back up against the sinks
and puts his face right there, I notice we're the only ones in
the bathroom. How the fuck does this happen?

Now let me make one thing clear. I'm not a tough guy. Not
a tough guy, not a fighter. And the reason I love legalized
casino poker so much is that you don't ever have to take it
outside the card room. Here's what came out of his mouth, the
wild-eyed slobber-jawed maniac. "Young fuckin' punk, you
think you're shit. Outside I'm gonna kill you, I'm gonna
motherfuckin' kill you, you little cockeyed piece of punk shit.
What you think . . ."

He didn't hit me. I mean I don't know if I think he was
gonna or not, he just had me there up against the sinks

grabbed by my arm and I'm scared and I'm just trying to talk my way out of it. Someone comes in and he lets me go and now I know that all of the sudden I got the advantage and I say, "Uh, sir, I feel you've got a lot of anger directed toward me. Uh, is this something you want to talk about?" Conflict resolution, that's me. The nineties kid.

And he sneer snarls wavers around and says he's gonna kill me and let's go outside, and I say, "I don't want to fight but I'm certainly happy to talk about this conflict we're having," and he staggers out the bathroom and I'm just standing there, just standing there with my heart going a million miles and I'm like, wow.

I ain't leaving the Mirage. There ain't no way I'm going outside the safety of this casino, don't take it outside the casino. Ain't supposed to have to take it outside. That's what we're paying all that money for.

I couldn't believe I really said that to him. Money gives you balls? No, sunglasses do. Image is everything. This I grew into. Put it right in my poker bag full of tricks. Question is, who I'm selling my image to, and what I'm selling to myself.

When you're winning at poker, you gotta figure to try and put some order in it somewhere. And that's where ledgers come in. Poker players keep ledgers because they need them. They need them to show that they got it all under control. But it's never under control. No matter how many wins you got in a row, no matter what your hourly win rate is, no matter what. A few things go this way or that way and you're sitting there counting your money, cursing under your breath, shuffling your chips, heart a-pounding, gasping for air, and making those questionable decisions when you're stuck in a big game after twenty-four hours wondering what the fuck's happening and why it's going on now.

Any talk about poker ledgers has to start somewhere with Larry Sandtrap. It's fair to say that for me he invented the damn things. Larry Sandtrap, mathematician turned poker pro, who came out with the book on Hold'em and limit poker in the late eighties and reduced poker to numbers and volatility and swings and bets per hour and standard deviations from the mean. I was all ears because looking at poker in this way made it professional, put me on the inside, made me feel like one of them. So I started to track my results, like sitting at home with a calculator on my bed adding up wins, always after a win, and how many and how much I was making and how much I was gonna make per hour and what my bankroll requirements are if I want to have an 87 percent chance of fluctuating only two standard deviations. I can tell you what drove me out of the ledger business. It was order and when I lost eighteen times in a row in 1994.

My Vegas roommate Al, whose ledger consisted of a huge calendar, he'd fill in the space for every day with a giant W or else an L, and the amount he won or lost. That's all. Any surprise why Al would try so hard to make sure he had a win? I mean he hated to quit a loser.

Yeah, everybody's got their own ideas about keeping a ledger, but one thing's in common—they're personal. I mean a guy might say to you, Yeah, I'm ahead twenty thousand this month, or, I lost six plays in a row, or, I've had pocket aces hold up sixteen times running, but you're never gonna see that ledger. People keep it to prove to themselves that they should keep playing, that they're ahead. Keep it under their pillow to consult like a Bible on those dark and stormy nights. Like anything on paper is gonna make sense of the chaos of the gambling world when your stomach jumps in your mouth and your heart's a-pounding and your eyes are darting and somewhere in a college professor's drone Larry Sandtrap, godfather of the modern-day professional, is saying, "The total number of hours played divided by the limit and result should yield one expected standard deviation per pot and a value of bets per hour in said game. . . ."

Al coming into the living room of our apartment on the twenty-second day of the month, proudly carrying his wall calendar, the square for every day taken up by a large W in thick black marker and the amount he won each day written in smaller figures. That was it, W and the amount. Not the hours he played, not the game, not where, not when, just the W and a number. Al loved to hit and run, he was the master of the twenty-five-minute poker session. Just get the W and go.

Wouldn't you know on the twenty-fourth day of the month I come into the Mirage poker room and there's Al playing in a 20-40 game. He almost never played higher than 10-20 but now he's stuck and been in the room thirty hours and trying to get even and I look around his table and see shark central staring him down and I go over to him and say, "Al, what's up," and he looks up at me with big red eyes and says in a hoarse whisper, "It's a good game." Yes, it is possible to go broke all in one day. It doesn't matter how many fuckin' W's you have.

FRESH
MEAT

FOR ME THE biggest problem with Bart Stone is always trying to figure out if the guy is for real. I guess it doesn't matter. I first encountered Bart up in Connecticut in the early days of Foxwoods, in 1992.

I'm playing 30-60 Hold'em and Bart strides into the room, comes over to the table, crashes into the one open seat, and bangs down onto the table—my first thought, a football—a seething mass of money. Imagine taking stacks and stacks of hundred-dollar bills, scattering them on the floor, then gathering them up in one armful like autumn leaves, crumpled and squished and every which way. Now bind up the pile with twenty rubber bands, so what's left is something like papier-mâché art, but solid hundred-dollar bills. Bart slams this wad, which easily exceeds the combined chip values of the other nine players, plus most of their combined bankrolls, down on the table and the message is clear. Fuck you all. I'm a mean motherfucker and I've got so much money and I couldn't care less about it or care to count it and let's gamble, boys!

And I say the message is clear, because I got it. But with Bart, the message is always clear. After two or three hands (about six minutes) he says, "Fellas, this game is too cheap," and he is up again in a whirlwind, parading around the room with his football of money under his arm, looking for action and looking mean as hell. All eyes in the room follow him, whispering, pointing, and wide-open jealous.

There were more opinions about Bart than there were people in the Foxwoods poker room. In the poker world, there's a lot of labeling that goes on—everyone's a face and everyone's got a rap or an MO. Live one, pro from California, solid but goes on tilt, broke, rich, good at Hold'em but terrible at Stud and Hilo, good at poker but blows money in the pit. Why? Everyone wants to know where the money comes from and who has it and who's getting it and how much it is. How much has he got? How's he doing in the big games? This is on everybody's mind that plays there every day. Why? Jealousy, greed, incomprehension—a first encounter with a 50-100 Stud or Pot-Limit Omaha game is enough to make almost anyone wonder what the hell is going on.

One thing about Bart, nobody ever knows how much money he has. Some days he has more money than God. Other days he's dead broke. That's what he shows. Bart lives by that maxim from *The Cincinnati Kid*, "The state of a player's bankroll is a well-kept secret." All I know is that you can't lose what is never shown, and Bart hasn't paid more than a few people that I know of and they all tell me he's broke. And I guess he sure acts broke a lot of times, with stories about football and craps and swearing to beat the band every time he loses a hand. And if he loses a buy-in then he leaves the table and paces around and talks to himself and leaves the room and then comes back fifteen minutes later and makes a show out of pulling another one or two thousand out of an inside pocket or deep down in his black sock in the black boot so the money's always crumpled. Then he throws it at the dealer so the game stops while Bart comes in for the minimum buy-in, and you could swear that this has to be his case money. But then the whole performance will be repeated again, several times if he's having a bad night.

Eventually he'll go on a rush, start winning every hand and chip on the table and you see the other Bart, wanting to play higher and stacking his chips in tall teetery columns. But I'm just telling how it happens, not what I think, which is that he has more money than God. But it's important to make people think he's always broke and losing so that he never has to pay them back and maybe they'll never catch on that he's robbing them. But I know he drives a brand-new white Lincoln Town Car and he ain't no idiot and he can play the spots off the cards when he wants to and read people just like a book.

Bart Stone always plays in the biggest game. He is always the center of the game. Bart sitting across a poker table—all eyes at the table, and most of the room for that matter, follow his every movement. Bart's Mexican, at least rumor has it that his mother was Mexican and he was born somewhere near the Texas border. But that's not what you notice most about Bart Stone. Bart always dresses in black—black pants, black shirt, black leather boots, sometimes with a big black hat. Bart always wears the same black bolo tie with silver tips, clasped up high with a small circle of polished silver. I'm always thinking he's got a third eye, a glinting glare just below the coffee-colored skin of his neck. Bart has at least twenty different black suede leather coats and jackets. And hard-coal eyes that make me shiver—or at least turn away. Bart is tall, well, not tall, but long and thin. Long arms, long legs, long thin black mustache. Bart, with explosive movements like a coiled spring and when you turn over a winning hand against him, Bart blows up. His legs give a jerk, the cards fly at the dealer or across the table, his head is moving, his arms are flying and it takes an effort not to hide behind your chair or raise your arms up in front of your face. You swear that some object or fist is hurtling across the table at you, but it's only air from the force of Bart's emotion and the curses zinging out of his mouth like machine-gun bursts in that voice of his.

His voice. The first time I heard Bart speak, I thought maybe he had laryngitis. Then I heard the story, that some guy heard from another guy from Texas who knows Bart from way back, because Bart has been known all around that border area for a long time.

Many years ago a young Bart Stone played a jeweler in gin rummy and beat the fellow out of all his money, plus his jewelry store. Broke, sick, and thinking that he'd been cheated, the jeweler got a gun, shot Bart, and left him for dead. Next the jeweler turned the gun on himself.

Well, the jeweler died instantly, but Bart, shot twice in the throat and left for dead, survived. Bart survived, but he lost his voice and remained mute for twelve years, until he was able to have an operation that restored the ability of speech, but not of tone. His voice is a dry crackling whisper that has no timbre but lacks nothing for emotion. Laryngitis with the slightest Spanish accent and a filthy vocabulary.

Motherfucker! Accent on the third syllable. Cocksucking whore! These are his favorites. But Bart can be charming, too, and funny. Really funny. I swear it's true. The man can make you laugh. When he's winning, he says one thing and breaks the whole table up. People want to laugh at Bart. They want to watch Bart. Everything he does at the poker table is forceful and with a flourish. Just the sight of him walking into the poker room, pausing to take a mile-deep drag off a Pall Mall cigarette, is plenty enough to intimidate the hell out of anyone.

When he arrives at a game, he crashes into his chair, bangs his money or chips down on the table so everything rattles, and when all eyes turn upon him he grates out, "Deal me in!" More often than not, his next words are, "Why you playing so cheap, boys? Let's get this game out of the dirt!" or, "Boys, let's gamble higher!" But in that border rasp, "higher" sounds like "hiiiiir," long, drawn-out, and one syllable rising up— then dropping down sharp at the end.

And Bart playing in those crazy Pot-Limit Omaha games, having every chip on the table and then going broke in ten minutes. Raising every pot, bending his head over at an angle down to the table when a big bet is made to him. Then he explodes upward, rasps, "Raise," and pushes all his chips out to the center of the table in one motion. When someone thinks for a long time in the face of Bart's raise and then folds, Bart throws his cards up so all can see he is betting on nothing.

Foxwoods' poker room is split over the issue of Bart. Half think he is the best Stud player in the room. The other half think he is one of the worst. And a craps shooter to boot. Everybody thinks he's a nut. A maniac. A lunatic. My opinion? Hmmm . . . back then he just scared the hell out of me.

One day Wayne comes over to me and says, "Bart is either one of the best poker players in the world, or one of the stupidest people alive." He tells me about a hand he observed in the 50-100 Stud game. It gets down to the last card of the hand and Bart is left alone in a large pot with another player. Bart bets a hundred dollars on the end and the other player calls, ending the hand. Instead of now turning his hand over so the dealer can award the pot to him or his opponent, Bart lets out an explosive "Motherfucker" and hurls his cards toward the muck, thus killing his hand and forfeiting the pot to his opponent without even seeing if his hand is a winner or not. As some of Bart's cards lay face up in the middle, Wayne can't help but notice what hand Bart had thought so little of that he was willing to concede victory without even taking the free look at the other hand that he is entitled to do by the rules—two aces. In Seven-Card Stud, many would consider this a good hand. I'll just say this. No one that I have ever played poker with would give up a two-thousand-dollar pot with aces when he was entitled to see for free if the opposing hand is stronger. So Bart is somehow absolutely positive he has a losing hand, or else he's just fucking crazy.

But man, Bart knows what's going on in that Pot-Limit Omaha game. Like catching Uptown Raoul out of line. Raoul makes a big bet with two pair when the flop comes two, four, ten of different suits and Bart raises Raoul all in because he knows Raoul's gonna be scared as all bejesus and begging like hell to split the pot. And sure enough, Raoul's over there quivering like a boiled egg and, "Er, hey, what you got there,

Bart? I got a big hand, man, but uh, you want to split it, Bart?"

And Bart raises up and withers Raoul with a look and hisses, "Nooo!" And then when they burn and turn the fourth card and Uptown Raoul's got them saucer eyes rolled up in his head with fear about all that money in the center, Bart motions to the dealer to hold it up and he rasps, "Hey, Raoul. . . . You want to split it?" And Raoul gurble gurbles up and down and turns over his ten-deuce two pair, and Bart flips over his hand and shows no pair three-five-six which is nothing but a busted straight draw. Raoul is a big favorite and Bart just played him for a fool by getting a free shot to win the pot and no shot to lose. At least that's how I saw it.

THERE ARE A number of reasons for a poker player to get a backer. If he's broke and can't put himself in action. If he doesn't want to risk his own money. Or if he is just looking for another guy to rob.

Hot Mama Earl first showed up on the scene when Foxwoods opened in March 1992. Sixty-something, short cropped white hair on a nearly bald head, bright eyes, he almost always keeps his head covered with a Panama hat. First time I saw him without his hat I didn't recognize him. They call Earl Hot Mama because he used to own a string of sex shops throughout the Northwest called Red Hot Mamas, and some guy who knows said that they are the best porn shops in the area so Earl did real well for himself, and he's a smart guy and nice as hell but a few years ago he sold the business and moved his family to Hartford, Connecticut, to begin his retirement. And I never got the exact story, but I figure that the thumb-twiddling life just bored him. But then Foxwoods' poker room opened and now there's a casino within thirty minutes of his house and it's nonstop action and he meets all the guys who fill a romantic void of ramblin' gamblin' men and he can sit down at a poker table and not get up again for two days except to go to the bathroom and have excitement, gossip, and companionship, and time stands still and there's no need to think in any terms other than up and down, aces and kings. So it becomes a very pleasant place to spend eternity. Because that's what time becomes in there. Not Monday, Tuesday, days and weeks, but forget it all and welcome to the monkey house and nobody ever asks you any questions you don't want to answer, just bet or fold, how much did you win or lose, and did you hear what Bart did today that crazy motherfucker.

So being that Bart is far and away the most exciting guy in the room and Earl is one of the richest, they kind of get together. Earl starts backing Bart, which means instead of sitting and playing with us Earl sits in a chair behind Bart while Bart plays and watches his hands—the classic backer's position. And there is no question that a person backing Bart gets their money's worth in terms of action and excitement, which is all Earl's really interested in I guess anyway, that and his pride. He doesn't want all the guys to think he's a sucker and he wants to be making money with Bart and he wants to believe he's in the casino for the same reasons as everybody else, but he doesn't know yet or just doesn't want to know that there are no guys and there is no peer group, just a bunch of desperately lonely souls trying to make a few bucks for themselves by fucking over others. People who bullshit with each other just because you have to say something when you see the same people every hour of every day but aren't going to tell them anything true about yourself or how much money you got no matter what, so it's so much easier to engage in idle chatter and heavy gossip.

If a guy were to back me, sit behind me and watch, he would get bored in about six seconds flat. It's not very interesting to watch a guy sit there and wait, wait, wait for a good hand and then bet and hope that some goon is stupid enough to call. What can I say, it may be boring, but I stand a reasonable chance of winning and despite all else I'm not gonna rob the guy. With Bart, however, you got action from start to finish. First of all you're backing a guy that looks and talks like the meanest toughest bad guy in every Western movie you've ever seen. All the big action in the room revolves around or through Bart. With the force of his personality Bart dictates what game is played, who plays, and how high.

So now Earl sits behind Bart and Bart sure gives him his money's worth. He plays tons of hands, gets involved in every type of bluff, gives the act with ribbing people, throwing cards, shoving chips, up and down, Pall Malls smoking, winning every hand and then losing every hand. They're a team—Bart the front man, the player, the decision maker, and Earl behind him, overtaken with excitement and idol worship and financing all their exploits as they get involved in bigger games like a ten-thousand-dollar freeze-out with

Mario the pizza man and some big Pot-Limit games. What does it matter but that Earl thinks Bart is the greatest player in the world?

He comes over to me when Bart's ahead like five or ten dimes in a game, a dime is a thousand dollars, and he's positively glowing, his eyes are sparkling, that Panama hat down on his almost bald, very round head, his five-day whiskers belying his age maybe and lack of sleep that is par for the poker room, his mouth ever chomping on the end of a big fat cigar that is always there but never, ever lit. I never found out if it's because they don't allow cigar smoke in the poker room or if he doesn't smoke at all and just likes the image but I suspect the latter and there's always at least three more cigars in his front shirt pocket, individually wrapped. From his seat watching Bart play the big game Earl's sauntered over to the 20-40 Hold'em, ostensibly to "check out how the little hurt and the big hurt are doing." You know, see who's winning and losing today and to hear some bad beat stories and who played the ten-five off suit. But really he's out to report—brag—about Bart, and when he's over at the table where I'm playing with all the regulars—Scott, Pod, Gail, Danny the donut man, Brad the shoe salesman who looks like Joe Montana, Lucas who owns a salvage yard—Earl's eyes are so bright and he's so excited and his step is so light that he looks like a little kid and not an older man. I'm only twenty-two and he's maybe sixty-five, yet in the poker room we're peers and so he can barely contain himself and he says, "Sometimes when I'm watching Bart, Mick, I think maybe even he doesn't know what he's doing. He's just so many levels above everybody else. He's just so good, Mick, and most people have no idea!" This is kind of in idol worship mode because Earl wants to believe that poker is wild and mystical and beyond the understanding of intellectual mortals like himself.

My friend and roommate Jimmy put it in perspective about two years later when he told me a story about one day down at the Taj Mahal when he was playing with Hot Mama Earl in a Hold'em game. Now Earl thinks Jimmy is some sort of superhuman, not on Bart's level of course, but possessing some special knowledge about poker that's way beyond him. At one point Jimmy does something stupid—I mean really stupid—like he calls before the flop with a hand that's way bad against a guy who maybe hasn't played a hand in a while. Calls the flop with nothing and then check raises on the turn with almost zero except maybe some twenty-to-one-shot draw that miraculously makes a straight on the river, so when he flips his hand over at the end everybody's eyes widen in disbelief, and the poor chump who Jimmy beat in the hand gets out of his seat to make sure he's not seeing things. And Jimmy is keeping on his cool-rider face, but inside he's laughing hysterically because he knows how lucky he just got. Jimmy's not the sort to rub it in or show his emotions and admit that he made a stupid play so he's just looking down and raking the pot, and meanwhile Earl is sitting across the table with stars in his eyes, enraptured, drinking it all in because he thinks he has just witnessed a world-class player making a world-class play and not an ordinary sod who just had a snake charm stuck up his ass. Later when Jimmy and Earl both happen to be walking to the bathroom together and they're out of earshot of the other players Earl says, "Now I understand if you don't want to give away too many secrets, but could you explain to me about that play you made with the ace-six?" And Jimmy wants to look Earl dead in the eye and say to him,

Earl, sometimes I just don't know what the hell is going on and I just do stupid things and get lucky. But Earl doesn't want to hear that and he says, "No, stop. Don't tell me. It's probably too deep to understand."

So Jimmy instead smiles and looks mysterious and says, "Poker is a very complicated game," which is what Hot Mama Earl wants to hear anyway and he walks away thinking Jimmy is a poker god and Jimmy takes a deep breath and goes to the bathroom and tries to figure out how he's going to get back the five thousand dollars that he's stuck in this 75-150 Hold'em game and how the hell is it possible to be losing in a game where everybody is playing so bad. But luck is strange and the short run in poker is very unpredictable, so even though he's tired from eight hours of poker and hurting and feeling like a good seafood meal and a nice cold beer and a long sleep, he freezes his face in his cool-rider mask and trudges back toward the table. But all anyone can see is a relaxed smile, dark glasses, and impeccable concentration. And Earl is able to walk away thinking poker is deep, mysterious, and romantic, wonderful to be involved in, and not base, crude, and filthy.

I LEFT LAS Vegas for Connecticut with about seventeen or eighteen grand which was all the money in the world to me and then a drive across country in my maroon Ford Taurus with a stop to see my friends, my poker home boys, in Chicago and a detour up to the northern peninsula of Michigan to raise some hell in the 10-20 games up at the Chip-In casino in Hannahville.

I guess things could have gone better. I got my head handed to me at the Chip-In and what with putting out money to rent a place in Connecticut and losing seven out of eight times in the early and wild 10-20, 15-30, and 20-40 games of Foxwoods, I was feeling real close to desperate. Especially when I walk into the Groton Savings Bank at 9 A.M. sharp after having played all night until I ran out of on-hand money and I withdraw twenty-five hundred dollars in cash, their maximum daily withdrawal limit. And the looks they give me, considering I haven't shaved in days and I deposited the money barely a week before and they are very new to the casino scene up in Connecticut and I wanted more and I never take my foot off the gas pedal for the fifteen-mile ride back to the casino and when I run into the building taking two steps at a time and I go into the poker area, there's a twenty-five-person list for the 10-20 limit I've promised myself that I won't play any higher than that until I can put some wins together and my bankroll can stand it.

So when I see there's a short-handed 30-60 Hold'em game going on, which I've never played before and there's no question that it's much too high for my bankroll to withstand a loss in, I think for about three seconds and sit down. To me everybody looks like a killer, a pro; shows how much I know, Hot Mama Earl is in the game. And when I pull out of my pocket not a gambler's roll of hundreds but a white envelope saying Chelsea-Groton Savings on it containing fifty-dollar bills which no one in their right mind would want as fifties are considered bad luck and they're never used in casinos, everyone at the table exchanges glances and licks their lips and thinks fresh meat. I have to tell you that at that point I sure don't feel like no professional poker player and if I was asked at the time to give a logical explanation of my actions I would simply say, Shut up and deal.

And that's what happened, and like a cat with nine lives—don't ask me how—but I landed on my feet and it wasn't smart and it's not pretty but after that moment life started getting easier and I stopped sleeping in my car and started booking wins and making flushes and aces hold up and laughing at the table and thinking how pretty the waitress is at the twenty-four-hour diner down the road where I have tomato juice and eggs or a burger every morning after playing all night and I get even for the month and then ahead. And as I start to become more relaxed in the poker room I want to make friends or have role models or just be accepted as a peer by all those ramblin' gambling guys who seem to have it together, and so one day after winning seven hundred dollars in a 20-40 game—a major major win—I'm cashing out and getting ready to go up to Providence for the night to party with my friend Sandy, and there's Uptown Raoul.

You see, I'd been feeling like a big Hold'em player, a number one stroker ace who's ahead seven hundred dollars in a 20-40 game and bullshitting with a fellow regular named Raoul Abdul, whose respect I want, sitting next to me. I want people to think I'm a rambling gambling man, too, and not some baby-faced kid who's barely legal and can't handle the money, the pressure, the action. And when I'm not in a hand I'm trying to act cool and listening to the stories at the table and being real unruffled about all the red five-dollar chips stacked in front of me and in the pot and around and Raoul's

calling me his buddy and saying we're fellow Heebrews and
he's only part Arabian and it's just a brilliant day and the
table is very witty and tongue-in-cheek and so when Raoul
says to me, "Shalom, if you ever go broke, you can play my
chips," I say back to him in a loud voice to be sure the whole
table will hear and see that I'm a real cool gambler, "Yeah,
Raoul, and if you ever need anything, all you have to do is
ask."

He smiles and his eyes get greedy and he says, "Anything,
Shalom?"

And I smile and say, "Yeah, anything, Raoul." Like it's no
big deal and I'm cool and thinking how good it is that when it
comes to money all the real gamblers are blasé and unfeeling
and have honor and guys like me and Raoul would help out
each other if one of us was down. But it's all the world of
theory, you know, what you say you would do if that happened and this and that and so a few hours later when I'm
cashing out Raoul comes up to me real close and confidential
and says in a low voice, "Hey, Shalom, you did good today,
huh?"

And I say, "Yeah," proudly and with a big smile and Raoul
says, "Listen, Shalom, let me hold a thousand dollars until
tomorrow, okay?" And I'm stopped dead in my tracks and my
heart slams all the way up to the roof of my mouth and I
think, Oh, fuck.

And I say, "But what about all that money you got on the
table?" And I'm thinking, and what about all those oil wells
and how you're so rich and you were going to be the one who
lends me money if I'm broke and I ain't got a thousand dollars
to give out to a guy who I don't even know his last name. Or,
oh yeah, I do know his last name—Abdul. And Raoul says

something that I don't even remember or didn't hear but conveyed the message that he didn't need the money, of course not, he had plenty of that, but just needed to hold it in case something happened and he'll give it back when I see him tomorrow and what's the big deal and like in a trance I hand this big fat greasy man wearing a plastic jogging suit who would easily be the odds-on choice out of a hundred people to most likely shoot someone in the back, I hand him a thousand dollars and he smiles and says, "Thanks, Shalom. Buddies, huh?" and slaps me on the back and goes back to the game and I slowly walk to my car and get in and think, What the fuck have I done? You idiot!

And then I yell in frustration and bang my head on the steering wheel and start driving up to Providence and chain-smoking cigarettes and talking to myself and as I drive out of the parking lot and go on to the highway it occurs to me that I might never see Raoul Abdul again and how I never trusted that much money to anyone let alone someone I don't even know. After about half an hour I calm down a little bit and rationalize my situation to this—I didn't win seven hundred dollars today, I lost three hundred dollars—the thousand dollars I gave Raoul is gone. . . . I can handle it, and never ever again will I lend any money to anyone. And I'm really stupid.

It's funny, but never did I think about how I'm gonna get that money back or what I'm gonna do to Raoul if he doesn't pay, or anything like that. As I was driving I instantly saw it as part of the game, like part of the rules, and I'd been stupid and I'd lost. In the casino it's just chips, red and green and black, and pots and money change hands so often and so quickly that you lose touch, you lose meaning. Because when

you're in action and you're winning you think, This is the way
it will always be and everyone around you will keep being
there every day in the same games with the same money, the
same smiles, and the same jokes, and if they need a few
dollars for a while you'll give it to them and if you need a few
dollars for a while they'll give it to you. Ain't life pretty?

What really brought it home for me is the look on Sandy's
face when later that night I told him what I'd done. "You
gave him a thousand dollars to gamble? What if he doesn't
pay you back? A thousand dollars!"

"Uptown" Raoul Abdul was already at Foxwoods when I
got there in April '92—or maybe we both arrived at the same
time. But the first thing I remember about him is that we're
playing 20-40 Hold'em in one of those wild games in the back
corner of the downstairs poker room that they later turned
into a slot parlor where it was always either full tropical
sweating hot or polar ice cold, depending on the air system,
off or on. I'm in the eight seat and Raoul's in the two seat
betting golfer Dave from New York on whether or not I'm
Jewish. But Uptown Raoul knows I'm Jewish because he
asked me a few days before and he calls me a fellow Hebrew
because he says he's "half Jewish himself on his mother's
side," which is about as believable as saying the moon is green
cheese because Uptown Raoul Abdul is about as Arab-looking
as the Sheik Farazzi. So when Uptown says with that devilish
grin when he's sitting there in his bright red plastic jogging
suit size extra beyond large to cover up his poker player's
paunch and then some, "Them bagels is good stuff, eh, Shalom?" when he cocks his full head of hair dyed in this weird
black—he's got to get a new dye, either it's cheap or he just

uses it wrong, it always makes his hair a reddish tone to go with his thick dyed mustache and dyed goatee—when he says, "So Shalom, you and me fellow Heebrews, eh?" there is just nothing to do except laugh.

They call Raoul "Uptown" because he never says, "Raise," instead he looks around with that devilish grin and says, "Ahh, we're going uptown!" or, "You took it uptown? You don't know how to go uptown! I'm taking it uptown! Let's gooo—uptown!"

Uptown Raoul calls me Shalom because of the bet he made with golfer Dave from New York, a New York Jew who plays poker on the weekends, every weekend or like Thursday through Sunday. He plays tight and puts his hours in and picks the good games and makes his money and in the early days of Foxwoods I'm just the baby-faced kid wearing the white floppy Wisconsin fishing hat. So Raoul says, "And Shalom here," pointing with his head as he stands up over the table to rake a pot with his greedy grubby big fat hands, "he's a Heebrew also. Right, Shalom?" With the big grin breaking out all over his face—he's always happy like a little kid in a candy store when he wins a pot—pure boyish happiness, and they bet fifty or a hundred bucks and then it becomes the talk of the table and the room, everybody laughing and Raoul keeps saying that I have to pull down my pants to prove it— that I'm circumcised. But he always calls me Shalom after that, and there have been plenty of after thats since then and we're both survivors, or at least still in action.

Like one night at Foxwoods playing 30-60 Hold'em all night and the game gets progressively short-handed as the night goes on and the winners quit and some people go broke and finally there's just me and Raoul Abdul and some chump who I haven't seen before or since—three of us stuck, tired, and refusing to quit. And we play on and on and I hadn't played much short-handed Hold'em at that time so it was chaos and we were all three playing every hand, betting and raising and playing fast and not talking and it's about three or four in the morning and there's only maybe two or three other games going on—small Stud games on the other side of the room—when right in the middle of everything, all the power goes out. And in that basement poker room where there's no windows, it becomes pitch-black—blacker than black.

Of course everyone's first instinct is to grab their chips, make sure their money is safe, and a minute or two later a few security guards rush into the room with flashlights. And after making sure that no one stole any money from the dealer trays—the dealers are all taught to lie on them in case of an emergency—they're just standing there, and now that the initial shock of all the power poofing has passed and it's not a robbery or nothing but just the inefficiency and inexperience of a new casino the three of us start thinking about how stuck we are and how we're paying time and hurry up and deal.

Like at the Taj Mahal in Atlantic City when Floyd has been playing seventeen or eighteen hours in a row without stopping to eat, sleep, or go to the bathroom because he's so fuckin' stuck he don't want to move. And finally he can't take it any longer so after he folds his hand he says, "Deal me in," and starts sprinting for the bathroom, which in the Taj isn't so close—no, you have to go out of the whole poker room and down the hall—and so the hand ends and the dealer shuffles and says, "Should I deal him in?" and Virginia says, "Yeah, give him a hand . . . he'll make it." And sure enough it hasn't even been thirty or forty seconds and you can see Floyd through the plate-glass windows separating the poker room from the hall coming at a dead run, full sprint, waving frantically so we can see that he wants to be dealt in and there's no way that the guy has time to finish let alone wash his hands, but when you're stuck you don't want to miss even one hand, not even after eighteen hours and five or six hundred of them. And it's not just Floyd—I mean we all been there. And I heard that's why Tom H got booted from the Stardust casino because the game was so rocking and wild and he didn't want to miss a hand and walk all the way to the bathroom so he went in a corner and pissed in a garbage can.

But so me and Raoul and this chump are just sitting there in the pitch-black and we really have no interest in being together unless it's to gamble and I got that feeling where if I don't get back into action quick then I'm gonna scream. And I don't know how Raoul pulls it but he does a little hell raising and cajoling and the next thing I know there's four security guards at our table—one for each of us including the dealer—standing behind our chairs with big powerful flashlights. And for the next twenty or so minutes we play Texas Hold'em like that—there in the pitch-black with flashlights shining down over our shoulders and on the table and now it seems funny or lunacy or just makes a you'll-never-believe-this but at the time, while we were playing, it was the most normal thing in the world. Or should I say just completely par for the course for Raoul and I, guys who for weeks and months have spent more time inside casinos than out. We weren't thinking anything at the time but Good, now we can play—and shut up and deal.

Not, Oh, my gosh but we're sickos, can't even stay out of action for five minutes, and it's like when people hear that I'm a professional poker player the bulk say, Yeah, yeah, yeah, you're so lucky because you can do whatever you want, play whenever you want, make your own schedule. But I know a lot of guys who play poker—hell, I feel like I know all of them—and to a man it's play poker, eat, sleep, eat, play poker . . . poker, poker.

And when I'm in the groove after playing for something unreal like eighteen or twenty hours and then home for five or six hours of fitful sleep and then pop out of bed, it's not relax, flip on the TV, go out to eat, call my friends, read a book, play golf, see a movie. But jump awake, run in the shower, convince myself I don't even have time to shave or finish listening to a song on the stereo, and run down to the kitchen and no time to cook a proper meal or even sit down and eat but whatever I can grab and run to the car and eat on the way. And fifteen minutes later, after running a few questionably yellow red lights, there I am back at the table like I never left, and as I look around it's the same everywhere— bleary-eyed and in action.

SURPRISE OF ALL surprises, but after a relatively sleepless night plagued by fitful visions of Raoul Abdul's leering face saying, "Buddies, right, Shalom?" I'm back in the poker room in another 20-40 game, or maybe the same one still going from yesterday with a mostly new crew, when who should walk in but Uptown Raoul. And without further ado he comes right up to me, reaches into his jogging suit's jacket pocket, and hands me a folded roll of bills—a thousand dollars.

"Thanks a lot, Shalom." And then he's off again, getting on the list, finding out the gossip, making his rounds, ordering a sandwich, lighting a cigarette. So for the second time in two days, Raoul stuns the hell out of me and I am happy to get my money back but I still know I want no part of being involved with him.

Not even three days go by before Uptown is back at my sleeve—"Hey, Shalom, let me have that thousand dollars back for a while, okay?" This time I say no. It's not easy—it's never easy, but it gets easier every time. Since then, Raoul has asked to borrow money from me no less than twenty times—or go partners, or hold money for a while, or anything. And a lot of other people have, too. And some guys I become friends with, good friends, and I trust them and maybe they're running a little bad and I'm running a little good and they say Can I just borrow a little money for a few days or a few hours and I say No, no, no, no, and I've lost a lot of poker friends like that, but after a while it happens over and over. So many people get stiffed and go broke, and you wonder, is it possible to have a real good friend in the poker room?

THERE WAS THIS guy from Ohio, his name was John Smiley. All I can tell you about him is that some people say he's the best poker player in the world. And back in the early eighties before there was a big poker explosion and the only guys playing for big money were sharks and cheaters—and most people were both—John went out to Vegas and he played everybody head up, one on one, which is his specialty. And he turned nothing into a quarter of a million dollars in no time. Then he went back to Ohio and to his little house and he did nothing but take cocaine until all the money was gone. But this story doesn't take place in the eighties. This is almost ten years later and John is broke in Ohio, on and off cocaine and treatment.

John's a completely innocuous guy, short with a big round potbelly and a round face with big thick round glasses and a balding head and he always wears big pullover T-shirts that accentuate his potbelly. The first time I met John Smiley was up in Connecticut and we were playing 15-30 or 20-40 Hold'em, but John is looking kind of short stacked and he is saying, "I'm waiting for my friend Phil to get here. He's bringing the money." Which is kind of a straightforward and funny way of saying it and I took an instant liking to John Smiley—but everyone does—and I remember when Phil walks in the card room and over to John having just driven eight or ten hours from Ohio and says, "This is some joint they got here, John. What game is it you're playing?"

And John says, "Listen, Phil, first I need some money. I owe Bruce here three hundred and I need a little bit to play." And Phil reaches into his pants pocket, which are the kind of brown I don't know what they're made of pants that you get in one of those malls in Ohio, and pulls out a roll of hundreds. And me, twenty-two and like wow, I think, Now the money's arrived and Phil is a cool dude here to put John Smiley into action because he's a world-class player. But Phil's partnership with John only has the pretense of a financial arrangement. All Phil really wants is to have some action and help out his oldest friend and come into the room in that romantic way and have his best friend the superplayer bust everyone in town.

But Phil also knows John really well and knows that as soon as John is left to himself he starts heading for the shit, and Phil makes it clear that he ain't gonna have none of that and he may say it's because of the money, but really he cares about John and watched coke rip away his life.

I've never seen John Smiley lose at short-handed Hold'em when he's straight. Of course it's not like I've seen him straight so many times, but there's no question as to his skill. He says the only guy he ever played with whose skill intimidated him was Bond, a real low-profile guy who played in the big big games in the eighties in California when they were playing so high that you just try to figure out the zeros—like three and six thousand or something like that—and apparently Bond just made all the money. But I don't know the inside scoop on that, just grapevine shit.

Maybe the reason I am so instantly awed by John is because of how we are introduced. Wayne, who I feel like is the greatest and smartest poker player I ever met and never compliments anyone's poker game, I mean he thinks just about everyone is a monkey, says to me, "This is John Smiley," and I'm like, "Hello." Apparently they know each other and then as an aside to me later he tells me that John plays Hold'em real well which, as I say, coming from Wayne is a major compliment.

Foxwoods' two-week-long poker tournament is scheduled to be under way in a few days, which is what John and Phil have come for along with a slew of others like Mike Caro, who is the tournament host and occasionally seen in the 50-100 Hold'em, the tournament trail regulars like Eskimo and the Iceman and Lloyd and the Wizard and Phil Helmuth and a bunch of players from Vegas who come for the side action and guys from New York State and Maryland. And it became a poker free-for-all for a while. Mike Sexton won the big boy that year, a ten-thousand buy in No-Limit Hold'em which ended up only being contested by twelve guys who could get together sufficient funds or were lucky enough to win a satellite.

One section of the poker room is set aside for the whole two weeks of the tournament for the higher-limit games. It's wintertime and being that Foxwoods is all alone way out in the boonies and there's really no place to go—the casino doesn't even have a hotel yet, it's still too new—the players who have made the trip here are adventurers and die-hards. Everyone pretty much has the attitude, Let's gamble, boys. And they're off.

It's the day before the official start of the tournament and they're trying to get a 50-100 Hold'em game started.

Foxwoods doesn't normally have enough players to start or fill
a 50-100 Hold'em, but the locals are tasting tournament and
it's making the normal 20-40 and 30-60 players feel like gambling higher. I've never played 50-100 before but people are
milling around and I'm feeling like a big man because I've
seen or played with some of the out-of-towners before and I
know everyone else and people are looking at me to see what's
going to be happening and my ego is leading my brain around
on a string. So one thing becomes another and now a table in
the corner is being filled and prepped to start a 50-100
Hold'em and people are locking up seats and I'm worrying
about whether I have enough money and I confide in John
Smiley that I've never played so high before and am worried
about running bad and he smiles and says, "Don't worry,
Mick. Phil and I will swap some action with you," which I've
never done before either but things are moving fast and it
sounds safer to me. I mean it's unlikely that John and I will
both lose so we decide to take 25 percent of each other and we
go in the hallway where we can figure the money out and
where the ATM machine is so I can get some more cash—
four hundred from one account, two hundred from another,
and I only got about fifty-five hundred on me plus about a
thousand available on bank cards. As this represents about 40
percent of my total bankroll, I am short. I'm gambling. Look,
poker's not about the guy who doesn't make any mistakes.

So we're standing out there in the hallway in front of the
ATM, sorting out money and who's got how much and I've
got that feeling where it's like championship game time and
the adrenaline's pumping and I am pumped and the three of
us troop into the room and over to the table and I buy in for a
ton of chips to mask my fear and short bankroll and fingers

trembling and I pray to the lord to pick up a nice sweet no-brainer.

And I do. I mean I'm there, I'm focused and within an hour I'm hit with the deck and ahead about twenty-two hundred dollars. Nice score. I've never had a partner in a game before, and to me it seems like a real romantic ramblin' gamblin' type of thing, you know, having a piece of John Smiley, Hold'em champion from all over, and for him to think so much of my game as to want a piece of me. I've arrived. I decide that I must finally be a world-class player. What a sad load of shit.

I remember one hand from that game. I have ace-queen and the queen hits the board on the turn. And Old Man Harry check raises me and I triple raise him with just one pair because there's Mario the pizza man in the middle on a flush draw or some shit calling all the way. And Old Man Harry, he has ace-queen also and we split the pot. Check check on the end. John pats me on the shoulder. "Nice reraise." I feel focused.

Phil chimes in from behind, "Why didn't you bet on the end, Mick? I knew you had the best hand." Phil always knows everything after the fact.

John started the night way down, but he came back and we both got even about the same time, which is when I quit. The game has gotten a little short and I am tired and a little bit pissed that my twenty-two-hundred-dollar start has turned into something like a two-hundred-dollar win, some of which I give to John to square our partners thing. So I quit and Phil and John barely pay me notice except to smile and John says, "Oh nooo, I'm not quitting this game until it's completely over." Now that he got even I guess he is looking to make something.

And Phil, for all those hours the perfect backer, sitting behind John and I, chain-smoking Marlboro Reds, congratulating, commiserating, handling the cocktail waitress, and engrossed in the game. "Yeah, see you later, Mick. John and I are just getting started." Deep drag on his cigarette. Well, I'm just tired and to me the game doesn't look nearly as good anymore and 50-100 just seems too big right now.

After that night the 50-100 Hold'em game went pretty often. At least during the two weeks of the tournament. It was a few days later I watched John Smiley play head-up 50-100 with this girl Jewel from Las Vegas. She plays good—at least I think she played good when I played with her in a ring game, but she's also as cold and mean as they can get, which I didn't know then but I know now, two or three years later after being in Las Vegas over New Year's Eve and I'm playing in a game of 50-100 Hold'em with her and Lollipop Boy, and I guess she's with him now.

But anyway, John and Jewel and some other people are at that back corner table in Foxwoods where the 50-100 game was—because it just broke—and Boston Scrag says he'll back Jewel against John. And John cleans Jewel out of all her chips in fifteen minutes flat. I guess she thought she could run over mild-mannered John, but John just beat her bad and then Scrag sits down and decides he's going to get even by playing John himself and Scrag proceeds to win three pots in a row on the river, the last card—unbelievably lucky and big pots, too, so he's almost even and he quits. Scrag never plays limit Hold'em and he knows it. He mostly plays Pot-Limit Omaha but he's kibitzing over here, maybe trying to impress the blonde. Anyway, John doesn't say much. He's completely mild-mannered, but he has to be a little pissed about getting so unlucky against Scrag. I just think, like Phil, that John Smiley's the best I ever seen. We're sitting there dying about it.

I REMEMBER THE first time that Jimmy and I swapped action. We had gotten to know each other the winter of '93, after the poker tables opened in Atlantic City the summer before. Jimmy and I just kind of gravitated to each other from the start, maybe because we sensed that in the poker world we're a lot alike. I mean, we try to be honest.

The first time we swapped action coincided with the first time I played 100-200. In poker that's how it is—people are always identified by what limit they're playing. Like when I visit Vegas and I say to Al, Hey, have you seen Danny the Dog lately? And Al says, I heard he's playing 30-60 somewhere. 30-60. Always the limit he's playing. So I'll know how much money he's got.

Like when I'm back in Vegas for the first time in like two years and some guy will come up and say, Yeah, man, we heard you're playing 150-300 every day. And I'm like, Whatever, man, I don't even know you, and I just stand and smile and say Yeah and Tsk, man, in appropriate places and thank God that I'm wearing my dark sunglasses.

So, yeah, 100-200 Hold'em—it's bigger than 50-100, which is what conservative logic would tell me to play, but I'm not worried about the lineup because Porpoise is gonna play and some guy who I've never seen before but he wants to gamble and won't play any lower than 100-200 and with any less than five people. And Bart's in charge. He gets it all together and Jimmy and I have a quick whispered conference and I say, "Jimmy, man, that's too high for my bankroll," and he says, "Yeah, I know, but what are you gonna do? It's gonna be a good game." Impassive behind his sunglasses.

And I say, "Look you want to swap some action to protect ourselves in case one of us runs bad?"

Jimmy says, "Yeah, how much should we do? A third? No, maybe that's too much. Mickey, you decide."

"Okay, we'll swap a third. Yo, man, just make sure you know how much you're buying in for and we'll figure it out later."

"Yeah."

"Yo, and uh—don't tell anyone, man."

We both felt bad about it after. When you're playing with five guys and you're swapping action with one of them you can't help but cross over that line. Like if I'm in a pot with Jimmy and another guy, and Jimmy bets and I think maybe I got Jimmy beat or maybe I got a good chance to win say with a heart or a second pair on the end and I know the third guy's on shit. And Jimmy bets. Well, I might raise in that spot, but with Jimmy and I swapping and I get one third of the pot if he wins and two thirds if I win so there's no way for me to lose money in the pot and now I'm good and goddamn for sure raising. But that is playing partners, it's unethical, it's . . . cheating.

See, but that's not how we're thinking about it. It's just like look, I'm comfortable with the competition but not the stakes. And no matter how bad the competition plays, you can still lose a lotta money, and quick. So I don't want to play that high. I want to know if someone who likes the way I play would like me to put some of their money in action for them at no charge. So while I'm playing at the 100-200 table, I'm only 66-132 and my partner is playing 33-66. But I'm making the decisions. So instead of losing twelve thousand dollars, I'll only lose eight. Or the other way around. And then Jimmy might want to do the same thing. So I take a piece of him because I like the way he plays. Yeah, yeah, yeah. Rationalize.

And I remember the last time we swapped action in the same game. It's the night I lost all that money wearing my maroon zoot suit and maybe there was a lot of weird stuff going on. Someone accusing Tofu Trina and the Fresca Kid of going partners and Crazy Roger backing Sportscar Bernie and everyone else or I don't know, but Caterpillar Jay stands up and slams his hand down on the table and says, "All right! If anyone at this table is partners with someone else, I want to know about it!" Jay, solid block of granite wearing a Caterpillar truck baseball cap, with a teakettle for a temper. Jimmy and I don't say anything. Don't even look at each other. Not that it really matters. No one can accuse us of cheating because we're both the two big losers in the game.

When we got home we decided no more swapping action in the same game. If you want to give up a piece of yourself, fine. But it's just too weird when someone else is involved. Poker is designed for every man for himself. No. That's just the fairest way to play it. But isn't everything fair, Machiavelli.

FOXWOODS, 50–100 HOLD'EM. It's the Christmas tournament, I'm just back into poker after four months in Europe, and I have a foolhardy desire to test myself against prime competition and gamble with my bankroll. So here I am—stuck—at three o'clock in the morning and it's a purple rope game.

Because of too many spectators crowding the big games during the tournament, the two high-limit games are cordoned off. It's completely superfluous now because there are no spectators. None. In fact, the casino is almost deserted. Our poker table is roped off with the things they use in movie theaters and shows, thick, furry, purple rope attached to gold stands, and now because the game is full and there's no spectators it looks like maybe the purple ropes are to keep the players in rather than the spectators out. It seems that way, too, because no one has moved from their seat in five hours and no one looks in a hurry to go anywhere except maybe New Castle Ted. There's something else, however, that accounts for the fact that no one's left this game and that the casino is deserted, and it's not the fact that it's three in the morning.

It's snowing. Hard. Like a blizzard. Rumor has it that the roads are impassable, so nobody's leaving. The ultimate poker game. Like a slow boat to China.

And like I said, Foxwoods doesn't even have a hotel yet—

they've only been open ten months—so nobody can even duck away to get a room. And it is a rocking game. There are guys in it who haven't played much Hold'em before. But I'm stuck, losing in the game, and Frank who is sitting next to me is stuck and New Castle Ted is stuck and swearing and calling everyone saps and the saps are getting lucky and the game is at a lightning pace. Everybody knows they can't leave, so they might as well gamble.

Afterward, Ted always says to me when we're in a really good game, They oughta get the purple rope out for this one. And it's funny, you know, because those ropes are purple velvet, like material for royalty, make you feel special, and inside the ropes is dirty gambling. So that you wish the ropes really are there to keep people in—to hold them or tie them up while you take their money and their watch. But right now those purple ropes with the gold stands are just around the table, about two feet behind all the chairs, and the game is hopping and humming with at least four or five guys in every hand and ten at the table plus the dealer and there's one other big game going at a table not far from ours, but it's definitely not full and they're playing Stud, 200-400. And there's Bart Stone and the Iceman, who won the World Series of Poker one year and a lot of tournaments since then, and maybe one or two other people who I don't know real well, but I do know, even from my position at the table so that my back is to him, that Bart Stone is losing.

Bart Stone. I can hear his motherfuckers and this and that and cursing the dealer from over here. But our game is humming and I don't pay it much attention because I'm stuck and tired and not really playing that well. Now New Castle Ted loses two or three hands in a row and he throws down his cards, picks up his chips and money, says "Lucky fucking saps," stalks over to the bigger game and takes an empty seat. New Castle is like that—he can't tolerate losing and he figures that if he's stuck a few thousand at 50-100 it'll be much easier to win it back quick at 200-400 than stay here . . . or else go broke. But he figures that he's such a good player that he's supposed to beat anybody as long as they're not too lucky.

Anyway, Ted's over there playing with the big boys now and I'm thinking his bankroll isn't really comfortable for even 50-100 but it doesn't really matter. The rules state that all you need to sit down in a game is the minimum buy-in, and in a 200-400 game that's only two thousand dollars, I think. But it can all be gone on the first hand—or not. That's New Castle Ted, always looking at the small picture, how he's doing right now, rather than at the game. I mean how could you leave a game like this? Not that I am doing any great shakes either because I'm sitting on Frank's right and we're bullshitting and talking between hands and he's always asking me what I had and every time that I raise he reraises right behind me and tries to isolate me and some of the hands I'm raising with are shit and some of the hands that aren't shit I'm missing the flops and maybe getting bluffed out, usually by Frank.

Frank, he's got my number and he seems to be winning a lot of pots lately, and every time I call him he's got enough and every time I fold he's got shit, but this is before I learned to freeze someone out and so it just seems like I'm giving Frank a lot of money. This is mainly on my mind and I'm thinking about how much I'm down and whether or not I should have played that ten-jack, or raised with it, and I'm not paying attention to much of anything outside the game and when New Castle Ted comes back over and takes the seat he recently vacated I almost don't notice him.

I almost don't notice him, but I do because the change in his personality and temperament is so profound that you have to notice the guy, along with all the chips that he definitely didn't have when he left the 50-100 game thirty minutes ago and now comes plopping back down for all to see. And he's practically whistling he's so full of gaiety and himself so that there's no reason to ask how he did. This time he got even— and better.

He's doing the eye-catching thing, which is what some people do when they have something that they want to say or tell to the whole poker table but know that nobody really wants to listen or they feel stupid talking to no one. You catch somebody's attention and then you can talk to them. Maybe I'm just easy. Guys are always talking to me at the poker table. Probably because I just sit there with a stupid smile on my face while they blabber away. There are some guys who I think play poker mainly because they want people to talk to, and the poker table is a good place for that. Ten people sitting around a table, unable to change seats and with no option but to be some sort of audience for whatever drivel a lonely bastard wants to spew. But Ted's also doing the chuckling thing, where he shakes his head as if in wonderment to himself and laughs softly, like he's just seen or heard something which is more funny or exciting than you can imagine and he can't wait to tell. But you have to ask.

So I say, "What's up, Ted," me the sucker, and he says, "You'll never believe what Bart Stone just did in that game. This has to be the all-time craziest fucking thing I've ever seen." So now I'm listening and a couple of other guys at the table prick their ears up and New Castle Ted has an audience, which is what he really wanted in the first place. Now he's made his little score for the day and he's feeling like chirping. Chirping chips, we say. A guy gets some chips and he starts to chirp. Now that Ted's ahead he's happy, doesn't really care about winning or losing so much and is in that winner's mode where everything is so funny and the poker room is filled with exciting characters and stories and interesting things besides the actual action itself. That's when you're winning. Ted tells us what he witnessed in the other game just five minutes before.

Bart Stone is losing. And he's mad. Real mad. After losing a brutal pot he looks like he's finally had enough. Bart jumps out of his seat hurling curses, picks chips and money up in one giant armful, and then throws chips and money back down on the table and hisses, "Deal me in!" just in time to receive his first card down from the dealer. Bart picks the card up and slams it back on the table face up for all to see—king of diamonds. Even the professionals at the table raise their eyebrows in mild surprise and amusement—they've been playing with Bart all night. Bart gets his next card down from the dealer and flips that over also without looking at it—eight of diamonds. His third card is a two, also diamonds, which I guess is a good start in Stud—three suited cards—but in Stud your first two cards are supposed to remain hidden to the end. Bart's whole hand is exposed. Stupid!

Since Bart's low with the deuce he's forced to bet fifty dollars, which he wings into the pot like he's trying to stone the dealer, who says deuce of diamonds is low. The Iceman, sitting across the table from Bart behind a mountain of chips and every hair in place, takes a sip of his mineral water and raises with an ace up. Bart reraises. Everybody else folds. The Iceman reraises, making the bet six hundred to go, and now Bart calls. The Iceman's representing aces, but does it matter? I mean he's playing a pot against a man who's showing him his cards. But Iceman does have aces and when the next card comes and the Iceman catches a blank and Bart catches the four of spades, which is also a blank, a nothing card, Iceman bets two hundred dollars and Bart calls, throwing his money in while still bending over behind his chair with a sneering snarling kill mask of rage, which is why nobody asks him why his hand is exposed. Everyone's just watching.

Bart's fifth card is the four of diamonds, which gives him a four flush and a pair. The Iceman catches what appears to be a blank, but if he's got aces then he's still the favorite, but a slight one, or so I'm told, depending on what cards he has in the hole and which cards have been exposed, which is something that I don't know. But I'm sure the Iceman does and what happens next is just way out for anything, way out, because now the lights are shining down on this poker table and there's green twenty-five-dollar and black hundred-dollar chips and lots of hundred-dollar bills in front of the players but there's only four or five people at the table plus the dealer and nobody watching and empty tables all around except for a 50-100 Hold'em game going on a few tables away. And on the other side of the room there are four or five lower-limit games going on, but they are quiet too, and it feels very empty in that big poker room with about forty tables and only six games going and the whole place sort of empty and hushed. Everyone's thinking snowed in and gamble and no one's railbirding, not even the big game where they're playing

200-400, and Bart Stone's putting on a show or something. But he's standing at the table and playing this hand and his cards are all face up, which is ridiculous because why would he want everyone to know what he has, the crazy mother-fucker? I mean there's already two thousand dollars in the pot what with the antes and bets and raises up until the fifth card, but Bart ain't looking like he thinks there's anything wrong with showing everyone his hand, he just looks tall and mean and he's standing there and not talking, just looking like an ax murderer. But when the Iceman bets four hundred dollars with ace-ten-nine showing and two cards down, Bart just rasps one thing—"Raise." But he doesn't say it, he hurls the words out of his mouth and puts the money in and then they both become machines. The Iceman raises four hundred. Bart raises four hundred. And back. And forth. The Iceman sitting there tan, short hair, impeccably cut, groomed, manicured, cool, ready, casually dressed in a polo shirt and slacks and loafers and sipping from a bottle of Poland Springs mineral water, separating eight black chips off one of the stacks in front of him and placing them in two neat stacks of four, signifying a raise. And Bart, tall, gaunt, dressed in all black and smoking hard on his Pall Mall cigarette, all explosive motions as his fingers quickly count eight hundred dollars from a pile of bills he holds tightly in the other hand. And he throws the money toward the pot and the dealer. Raise.

The pile of money and chips in the center of the table that is the pot gets bigger and bigger, the dealer frantically trying to keep up with the action, until he realizes that something weird is going on here. So he just stops and waits and watches. Back and forth, Bart Stone then the Iceman—raise, raise . . .

Ted says they raised eighteen times until the Iceman finally called because Bart just wouldn't stop and they each had put like eight thousand dollars in just on that one card so there is about eighteen thousand dollars in a big pile in the middle of the table and there are still two cards to come.

Bart wins the pot. He makes a king on sixth street for two pair, now he has the best hand. Bart bets and the Iceman just calls and says wryly, "Aren't you going to turn this one over too?" to which Bart grates four hundred dollars and bets before seeing his last card. But the Iceman can't beat Bart's open two pair so he mucks his hand and Bart rakes a pot, which is like all the chips at the table, or at least all the Iceman's chips. Bart standing there like the Tasmanian devil, everything moving, wild, flailing, huffing, snarling, mean, lean, smoking, mass of anger. Except that his cards are face up, which in baseball is kind of like pitching to the guy underhand. Ted is laughing as he tells it and says Bart is one crazy man. I think it's wild.

FUNKY

WHEN I LIVED in Vegas it was either jogging suits or grunge, walking in in a pair of ripped jeans or cut-off shorts with a ratty T-shirt. At Foxwoods, Connecticut, I would never be seen without my Wisconsin floppy fishing hat. But it all changed when I got to Atlantic City and got a real poker wardrobe.

I moved down to Atlantic City in July 1993, and my clothes really began to take on a life of their own. I mean I had always been struck by the significance of the impression you give off. And for a long time now I had been kind of ill about what casinos are, how dirty they are underneath the glitter, and how there really is no dress code, only a money code, and I don't know but everything kind of went together. It was the nineties and grunge was about to be big. But I was finished with grunge just like I was finished with those silk and nylon jogging suits. Then I discovered the Salvation Army out on the Black Horse Pike. That's where I got my first seventies suits and a lot of weird stuff after that.

It was my friend Sal who first turned me on to the Atlantic City Salvation Army. All kinds of clothes could be bought there, he said, for nothing but a song. When I got there and saw all the stuff people had discarded that was out of fashion with stripes and plaids and polka dots and bell bottoms and fake velour and polyester, I felt like I was home. And all I knew was that I was going funky.

D URING THE FIRST few months of poker in Atlantic City, the summer of '93, being a poker player was like romping through the candy store. You would never believe that people just had that much money to blow. A lot of people won. Me, I always think about the monkeys and the typewriters. A long time ago I heard this story that's always stuck with me.

Take a monkey, sit him down at a typewriter, and let him bang away at the keys at random. Stick a piece of paper in, and see what happens. Most of what he types will be gibberish, but in there among all the "xzfl*" and stuff will eventually be a word or maybe even a sentence that makes sense to you. Take more monkeys, give them each a typewriter and more time, and chances are greater that one of them will come out with something recognizable. And if you take an infinite number of monkeys and an infinite supply of type-writers for an infinite duration of time, somewhere at some time one of the monkeys will type out the complete works of Shakespeare without a hitch. Of course there will also be many times more monkeys who might only get part of the way there—"The quality of mercy is not strkkvncxiotaeds . . ."—something like that.

Big deal, you say? That's unless you're a poker player, because I can't tell you how many people I know who managed in a poker sense to write *Macbeth* or *Romeo and Juliet* without any apparent effort whatsoever. Or maybe they only made it through Act IV. . . .

I GUESS YOU could call them the nouveaux riches. I mean they looked like everyone else, they played like everyone else, and they came into Atlantic City on a shoestring just like everybody else. But they just couldn't seem to lose.

Like Jerry. Jerry was a small guy, thin, thirty-something, and fond of wearing the jogging suits that they sold upstairs in the Taj's gift shop for a price that had one too many zeros in it. Now that I think of it, during the two months that we played together I never saw him out of one of those Taj Mahal track suits. Probably because he never left the Taj Mahal. He arrived on July Fourth weekend in 1993 with his little overnight bag and just never checked out. He told me that his weekly hotel bill was averaging something like two thousand dollars. This was before they were giving special room rates for poker players and when all your meals, room, clothes, laundry, and toiletries and whatever else are computed twenty-four hours a day in the unreal world of casino prices. Meanwhile, I'm paying five hundred dollars a month for an apartment two blocks from the beach that's less than ten minutes from the casino and can sleep about six. I have to admit it was a tad filthy. But just about every poker player in town was hankering to crash there.

Jerry was Indian, when he won a pot he'd say, "On behalf of my country, let me welcome you to the Taj Mahal!" White teeth grinning. Yeah, right, I'd like to hear what they say in Delhi, when he shows up wearing that Taj Mahal jogging suit.

What always struck me most about Jerry, though, were his eyes. They were big, but way sunken in their sockets and it always made me feel creepy, like I was staring at a skeleton. Most people thought he was a nice guy. Who wouldn't be a nice guy when they were winning something like twenty dimes a week?

I thought he was a pain in the ass. For one thing he talked too much. About what? I have no idea, but I can tell you for sure that he just never stopped. Bullshit, bullshit, bullshit. But me, I'm the guy with rocks in my head because I always tried to sit next to him. It's just that when someone plays as bad and as fast as Jerry, raising every hand, the best place to be is on his immediate left where you can control him a little bit, isolate him. But does it matter when no matter what anyone has or what anyone does, there's Jerry! Pulling out a miracle on the last card to drag down the pot, giving his goofy laugh, flashing his brilliant smile, beginning a diatribe on the technical complexities of the hand, asking, Whadidya have? Completely oblivious to everything. Insensitive, offensive.

And there's me, the moron, sitting next to him. Clamping my teeth, holding my tongue, and praying he'll stay. But he always stayed, and I was usually the one that quit crying. He could really play some marathon sessions—two, three days, no problem. I guess when you don't have anywhere to go but upstairs to your little room and then back down again and no one to talk to but your fellow players and no worries about losing, then it's easier to just sit and sit and sit. And no change, really. I mean he would continue to play as bad as always, talk and talk, drink his draft beers, and win. The only noticeable difference was his eyes. The more he'd play the more sunken they'd get. Sometimes it looked like those sockets were three inches deep, and when he looked at me big and brown, no matter how happy he acted and how much he smiled, I would always think of the character from *Fools Die* by Mario Puzo, who shoots himself after winning a million dollars. It sure gets lonely in casinos. No, that's not it. Casinos sure are the place for lonely people.

PHIL AND JOHN Smiley came breezing into Atlantic City the July that poker was legalized there. The Taj Mahal casino was the place to play, and the action was as wild as it gets. Phil was still backing John. Phil, a thirty-something well-built guy with glasses and uncombed straight sandy hair, chain-smoked Marlboro Reds, taking the deepest drags possible and then using his cigarette for gesticulating, punctuating, and giving the appearance of deep thought and profundity.

"Ya see, Mick"—deep drag and exhalation—"me and John here are looking to get him set up in a heads-up match. That's John's specialty. As long as he stays off the shit, John's the best player in the world."

Phil sits right behind John, watching John's every move while he plays, like a trainer for a world-class athlete. Meanwhile, as soon as Phil leaves the room John orders a Sambuca and downs it in one gulp—"Don't tell Phil—or is upstairs smoking a joint—"Don't let Phil find out"—or setting up a drug deal with some guy in a whispered conference in the corner or raising blind or putting a towel around his head so he can't see his cards. It's like a game they play. John Smiley has to stay drunk and fucked up and raise blind as often as possible and Phil has to stop him and play mom and keep John focused and handle all the money and not go broke while John tries to.

Ah, but that's just half the story. No, not even, because I remember the night when Barry B, bookie from New York, agreed to play this fumbling and pudgy and balding guy head up 150-300 Hold'em and everyone trooped over to Resorts because they didn't want to spread the game for two people at the Taj Mahal. So there they are, John, Phil, Barry B, and his flunky and John had agreed to let me have a third of his action and there was almost a problem because Barry B only had orange thousand-dollar and gray five-thousand-dollar chips from the Taj Mahal and Resorts wouldn't cash them. But then I come waltzing in wearing a purple polyester shirt underneath an olive-green army jacket, sunglasses, my hair cascading down everywhere, and I whip out neat little five thousand-dollar packets of hundred-dollar bills from my pockets and change his chips and I feel like a hustler and a big man. And then I sat over in the 10-20 Hold'em game while John Smiley cleaned Barry B out of eleven grand so fast it made your head spin. That night John was nothing short of awesome—focused, powerful, and well, just awesome. Then we divvied up the money and smoked a big joint up in my car—me and John, don't tell Phil—and laughed and went down and sat in the 50-100 Hold'em at the Taj feeling like everything was great. And I was so stoned I could barely tell the difference between sixes and nines.

I'm out to Chinese food dinner with Phil and John a couple nights later to celebrate. Phil and I are still riding high and we go to a restaurant outside the casino. Usually people that only know each other from poker rooms have a strange time outside of the casino, but John and Phil are fun guys to hang with. Toward each other they act like they're still in grade school. The deal is that Phil's old man made some money and his two sons help run the business and I guess they'll inherit it when they're not off gallivanting around in all the poker games in Ohio. And Phil's father even runs a weekly home game and Phil is taking trips to Connecticut with John to back him or Atlantic City or Las Vegas. Phil likes to play, too, but he knows he's not as good as John. Or he just prefers to back John.

Me, Phil, and John going out for a little Chinese. "What is this shit? I can't eat this stuff, man." Phil doesn't really have a taste for Chinese food.

"Just try it, Phil, and you might like it." John sounds like *his* mother for a change. Talk is poker, John telling about the days when he had all the cash and no one would play him head-up Hold'em, or when he was playing 800-1600 with Sand Man and Jowl Boy, two of modern poker's founding fathers or biggest hustlers. I'm hanging on John's every word.

Phil's like all over the place, man. I think it's a scrapyard his father owns in Ohio, and they come to the Taj Mahal the next weekend, all of the family. I see them all grouped around Phil's father in the poker room, explaining what's going on and pointing out John, who Phil is backing and is like one of the family anyway and tonight even the old man has got a piece of John. So John's sitting there concentrating and trying to play good and tight, which is not John at all and his heart is completely not in the game, but it's 75-150 Hold'em, a ring game and not serious and wild as all hell. When the troop goes off to dinner, John grabs his chips and goes with them.

Raoul Abdul showed up in Atlantic City, where he took up his usual position as eel of the poker room. I've had a chance to see all sides of Uptown Raoul. I've also played a lot of poker with him. He plays fine, and when he's winning he plays good, but he cracks easily and hates to lose and goes on

tilt when he gets stuck and plays every hand and starts throwing cards and cursing dealers and muttering to himself, and
written all over his face is a deep hatred for everyone in the
game.

And he's so childish, like slowrolling when he's got the
nuts. Some guy calls him all the way down and he'll say, You
got me. And even though it's his responsibility, it's the rule
that he has to turn his hand over first, he'll just sit there and
make his face all unhappy like he was bluffing and knows he
lost the hand. This is after the hand is over, you understand.
So it's just gut money, blood money. And then when his opponent flips over his hand and reaches for the pot, Raoul smiles
and acts shocked and says, Oh, I thought you had a flush, and
flips over his three of a kind which everyone knows is the nuts
anyway and you think, How can a guy be so needlessly un-
friendly? But I've seen Raoul do it all.

Like when he convinced some guy to go partners with him
in a 75-150 Hold'em game. They each put up a thousand
dollars and then Raoul played with the money. The guy was
standing right behind Raoul most of the time, but every time
he'd walk away to get a drink or go to the bathroom, I'd see
Uptown take a few green twenty-five-dollar chips off the table
and stuff 'em deep in his pocket. By the time they lost all
their money on the table, Raoul had managed to steal four or
five hundred from the same guy he ate dinner with that
night.

But there were a lot of guys in AC worse than Raoul. Once
I knew to say no to him every time he asks for something and
to always watch him like a hawk when we're at the table
together, I didn't get bothered so much by all the deviousness
he comes up with to stay in action. He's always in whispered

conference with some guy, or playing with this guy's money, or partners with that guy, or borrowing money from whoever is pumped up or too naive to say no. Maybe the reason I like Raoul so much is because I've managed to come out ahead with him. No, not ahead, but at least not out in the cold.

Raoul's got a certain level of poker-room charm. He can make people laugh when he's winning. And he plays the money real close to the chest, never shows what he doesn't want you to see. Some days he's playing real high and some days he plays low and some people he tells Man, I got boxes just filled with money! or some shit about oil wells somewhere, and some people he tells, Broke, man. I'm broke. Depending on who you are and whether or not he thinks you want to borrow money from him—fat fuckin' chance—or if he can put the tap on you. But he's got a good gig going. I mean I think he's got credit in a lot of places.

So I'm not too surprised when he pulls his grand coup. Raoul becomes buddy buddy with Poodles, a guy who comes up to play high-limit Hold'em during the week. They go out to dinner a bunch of times and Raoul borrows a few hundred and pays him right back and is straight with him for a few months. Then one day Raoul calls Poodles over when Uptown is at the cashier cage opening his safety deposit box. He shows Poodles that there's a lot of rolls of hundreds inside so Poodles knows he's got a lot of money. But really they're piles of one-dollar bills with one hundred-dollar bill on the outside, so instead of having twenty or thirty thousand in the box Raoul's only got four or five hundred. When they're out to dinner later, Raoul asks to hold ten thousand—just until he can go back to his box to get it. Poodles obliges and then Raoul puts him off for two days and skips town. And he picked a good guy to rob because Poodles isn't the kind of guy to do anything about it. But I'll tell you this, it's four years since I met Uptown Raoul, and he's still in action, and if you want to know how many other guys I know from back then who aren't broke, well, they can all be counted on one hand. And the other guys make Raoul look amateur.

PEOPLE ALWAYS WANT to know what's going on and what's going on is people are going broke. That's mostly it. And the trick is not to be one of them. I guess it's a little like musical chairs. Like that foot doctor from north Jersey named Roy or Pat or something who you see every weekend for like three months and sometimes during the week, and he always plays in the big game and craps and maybe blackjack and usually smiling and talking loudly about whatever, and one day he borrows a few thousand for a few minutes and no one sees him since. And Crazy Roger and Russian Alex and Jimmy are stuck with the markers because they're the easiest touches.

Eventually Jerry left the scene. He worked in a bank before he came to Atlantic City and he's a banker now. And about eighteen months after he disappeared from the scene he came back to AC for a weekend with his new wife and full of smiles and saying hi to all his old friends. It was just a little nostalgia trip for him and he comes on like those months in AC are just fond memories, so I have to think he didn't get hurt too bad.

Like maybe he just lost what he had already won or maybe he's just doing well now and so much happier that he forgot all about his stormy end. All I know is that after seven or eight weeks of torturing the games he started to play Pot-Limit Omaha. And all I can tell you about Pot-Limit is that luck doesn't get you very far, not compared to limit poker.

There were about three or four days when Jerry played Pot-Limit Omaha in a rocking game over at a table by the window. There were a lot of faces that dropped in and out of that game, but the only ones who mattered were Jerry and Bart Stone. They always cranked up the Pot-Limit Omaha at the table closest to the big-pane glass window separating the poker room from the hallway at the Taj. There was always a big crowd outside with their faces pressed up against the glass, and it's no wonder because it sure was a sight to see. There sat Jerry on one end of the table, white-toothed and hollow-eyed, looking small in his jogging suit and sitting on three cushions so that his feet didn't touch the ground but just dangled there, bare, a few inches above his penny loafers. There were chips in front of him but what no one could take their eyes off of was the pile of money that was stacked on the table in front of him—all hundreds. The money was lying there in one neat pile, but without rubber bands or wrappers or anything that separated, organized, or counted it. It was just there and the pile was no less than eight inches high, maybe more.

I'd walk outside and all that the spectators would be talking about was how much money was in that pile—forty, fifty, sixty thousand, I'm not really sure myself. But I guess he just wanted to have the most money on the table or maybe it was just an ego thing, but he sat there for I don't know how long, two, maybe three days, and Bart sat with him. Bart at the other end of the table, dressed in all black with his black hat and black mustache and cigarettes and fearsome and imposing, always trying to push up the limit. And I wasn't there to see it happen but eventually Jerry and Bart didn't want to play with everyone else, so they went next door to Resorts where they played head up, and I don't know how high they played, but I know that Bart beat him bad and Jerry left town the next day, and I didn't see him again for eighteen months.

Bart doesn't talk about it, but he broke him. I can't be sure but what am I supposed to think when you see Jerry every day for two months with sixty thousand on the table and then one day he and Bart disappear to play head up and you never see Jerry again but Bart's still there every day and a few weeks later he buys himself a brand-new Town Car and wants to play four and eight hundred with all comers. Yes, it is possible to go broke all in one day. No matter how much you have.

LORD, WHAT A night. A confluence of the moons or something, but everybody is in town—Iberville Tom and Floyd and Lester and Crazy Roger and Wiggy the cheater—and there are two big games going right next to each other. One of the games is half Hold'em half something else, but the lineup is kinda tight and so I'm playing in the juicy game, the action game. We're playing 100-200 half Stud Hilo and half Stud— the game changes every half hour—and I have never played

Stud Hilo before except twice $1-4 limit at the Mayfair Club in New York City, and here I am playing it one and two hundred. But I figure that I'll play real tight and that there are some people at the table who will play even worse than me. I'm wrong and I'm right.

First of all, it's not possible to play real tight if you play bad. It is possible to get lucky and win a lot of money, but it's not possible to play tight. But there are people at the table who play worse than me. Well, at least I know the rules.

Nobody at the table really knows the game except for the Fresca Kid, who is the reason we're playing the game in the first place, except that if you ask him he'll explain that it's really Lester's idea and everyone wants to play and it's the best game and all right already! Fresca Kid—shit, he's like a lawyer. But he's really one of the best Seven Stud Hilo players that there is and I guess he cut his teeth on the Seven Stud Hilo games in Vegas back when they were so tight and tough there wasn't any money around and everyone was cheating except for Fresca Kid, who's proud of the fact that he only had one losing month in four years and it was surrounded by huge net months on either side to cushion the blow.

So we're playing Stud Hilo—me, Fresca Kid, Floyd, Lester, Johnny World, some other dude, and it's a rocking game but then Josh Vasaki comes in like a whirlwind and throws a pile of money down and sits down in the open seat and stands up and then sits down and then gets up on his knees and lights a cigarette and says, "Deal me in. Hello, boys, what are you playing? Let's raise the limit. Yo, World, Johnny World, I want to play you head up, World. Fresca Kid! Kid, Kid, Kid, how's it going? You think you're the king. They say you're the best, Kid—I'm gonna beat you, I'm gonna break you, I'm gonna take all your money, Kid. Who's it to? Is it to me? Raise. I raise! What is this game, it's eight or better, right?"

And he went on and on like that, never stopped talking, never stopped moving up and down and fidgeting around and basically we all just smiled and ignored him, so that maybe I should explain about Josh Vasaki.

You might not believe that this person exists. Josh Vasaki is always broke—always broke—like it's his calling. And I'm reminded of a story my friend Kim told me about a guy in New York gambling circles by the name of Willy G. It seems Willy had a reputation for always losing and for never paying people back, and one time after Willy G won big in a poker game, which almost never happened, a guy asked for repayment of a loan and Willy said with complete sincerity, "But I don't have to pay you back. I'm Willy G."

Josh is like that. Well, of course he's broke, he's Josh Vasaki. He may be the most addicted gambler I've ever met. He looks like a guy who is losing the battle to look young, but fighting hard. His curly blond hair is just starting to recede a little on top and his body looks like once muscular now flabby and a growing paunch. But he's an all right enough fella to look at, I suppose—until you get to know him.

What makes Josh special. Not only is he known for always being broke, but he can run nothing up into a lot of money faster and more often than, well, I don't know, fast. But he never stops until he's broke. Never. Never sleeps. Just bets higher and faster until he's lost it all and then he starts again, the next day . . . broke.

And I have to think to myself, There is a man on cocaine and probably yes, what does it matter? But I mean it's just Josh Vasaki and behind him are two other guys who are brokes or broker than him, but because Vasaki's got money right now they're following him around hoping to get some. Big greedy eyes and broke everything else. Sure enough, someone lent Josh fifty dollars this afternoon and by playing poker and going to the pit and baccarat and higher poker and roulette and more baccarat now he has seventeen or eighteen thousand, and so now he's playing one and two hundred and betting a thousand dollars a hand blackjack when this morning he didn't have anything. Zero. Maybe a suitcase, maybe a change of clothes. And tomorrow he'll be broke—or whenever he goes to sleep. He'll never stop gambling if he's able to continue. And casinos are never closed as long as you still have money, so isn't that convenient and what chance does he have?

I guess bad stories about Josh abound. Todd says that Josh Vasaki is the only guy that can get a hooker to take him home, fuck him, and then give HIM money. And this is no allusion to charm or sexual prowess, but more like most unbelievable low-down con man in the world. Like I'm getting the money tomorrow, or this guy's check, or I just need the credit card for security to hold the room. Or when Josh asks red-headed Erik the slot machine junky if he can take a shower in his room and runs up a two-hundred-dollar phone bill and tries to get a cash advance charged to the room. Or Josh Vasaki bursting in on Jimmy when he's asleep and saying, I just need five thousand for twenty minutes, and Jimmy, real groggy—and I haven't exactly been able to figure out this part of the story—says yes and gives him the five thousand and Josh leaves and Jimmy lies there for a few minutes and wakes up a little bit and starts to wonder why Josh Vasaki needs five thousand for only fifteen minutes and why he gave it to him and he jumps up, throws some clothes on, and runs downstairs. There's Josh at the baccarat table with all his chips pushed to the center, betting everything on the hand, and Jimmy goes over and Josh only has fifteen hundred left and he's already bet it all and Jimmy has to stand there and sweat the hand and Josh wins and Jimmy grabs the three thousand and goes upstairs and feels lucky to have gotten the three thousand back and Josh acts like it is all natural and yes, isn't Jimmy happy to have the three thousand back?

Josh says "Oh baby" a lot. He reminds me a little bit of Gary Carter—you know, curly-haired and boyish, but with a little more flab. Every time he wins a hand it's "Oh baby! Oh baby! Oh baby, yeah!" He's having fun—like a little boy. There is no question that Josh is happiest when he is gambling.

Usually Josh wears a T-shirt and shorts, like he's at the beach. And thongs. And when you live in the casinos and are always crashing in someone's room or using someone's comp, then always being in the climate-controlled casinos may as well be the beach. And in that big white T-shirt his stomach makes a perfectly round paunch so he looks, well, he looks a little foolish. Look who's talking.

Seven Stud Hilo is a tricky game. Since it's possible for the highest hand and the lowest hand to split the pot, it's possible to catch someone in the middle. Two people who know they're both winners keep raising in order to punish a third player tagging along.

Floyd, Josh, and I are three players left in an already big pot and I have a low hand made and since Josh and Floyd both have high cards it looks like I'm guaranteed half the pot. I'm raising every chance I get. So is Josh. He's got two tens showing and he's making a hell of a lot of noise. He raises every bet, but Floyd is stubborn, calling all bets and raises. Josh is really animated. "Oh baby! Oh baby! Let's go! Let's gamble! What could I have? I know you ain't got nothing, Floyd baby, so I'm gonna bluff you, I'm going both ways, I raise! You raised, Mickey? Raise again! Oh baby!"

He's really excited. We cap the pot on every street including the last one. Josh has four tens. Holy cow, he really is running hot. I've got a low and poor Floyd was stuck in the whole time with three kings that never improved. Josh and I split a pot that's over twelve thousand dollars but a lot of it is our own money. Whew. That was a little scary.

"Four tens, baby!" He's up, he's down. "Let's kick this game up! Who wants to play two and four hundred? How about one fifty—three? This game is slow. You guys play too tight!" Josh is on his knees on the chair. Josh grabs a handful of bills from his pile and heads for the casino pit, flunkies in tow. "Watch my chips for me, boys. Oh baby!"

We all speculate on how much he took with him, how much he's got left, how much he's ahead in the game. Yes, he's actually winning. It's not allowed to take money off of the poker table but we're not gonna say anything for fear Josh will take all his money over to the dice table. Joe from Vegas, another broke, comes running into the poker room. "You should see Josh now. He's playing craps two thousand a number. He's stuck eight thousand already!"

Josh comes back into the poker room. Now there's about five guys behind him. He strides purposefully over to the table. He's the center of attention. He makes to pick up the rest of his money, then seeing the dealer about to deal the next hand he says, "Deal me in." He sits down, stands up, puts a knee on the chair, antes, raises, lights a cigarette, raises until fifth street and then calls all the way down, loses the hand, picks up his remaining cash and chips—about fourteen or fifteen dimes, my best estimate—and "I'll be back, boys," and beelines back to the crap table or the baccarat pit. One hour later someone reports back that Josh has gone broke. No one is surprised. We just keep playing.

PEOPLE ARE ALWAYS talking about golf at the poker table. It seems the two go hand in hand. And golf, like poker, is an excellent thing to bet on. I'm completely hopeless, like miss-the-ball hopeless, like I average 150 hopeless. Which is fortunate, in a way, because it's hard to imagine me getting hustled at it. But that doesn't stop guys from asking. Syracuse Don is always trying to get people to play golf with him. He wants to bet that he can shoot a 90 using nothing but his nine-iron. Apparently he can do it, too. Jake told me that Don shoots one of the best nine-irons in the country—whatever that means.

Bart's always going out to play golf with people, if they'll bet high enough. I've heard from several people who have played with him that he stinks—well, comparatively. Hot Mama Earl told me Bart would be lucky to break a 95. Bart and Grouse went out to play golf one day, and I've seen Grouse play and he's real good—low 80s or 70s. I don't know what happened except that Grouse lost twenty thousand.

Ouch. Funny thing is that when I heard the news I wasn't surprised at all. Just a little shocked that Grouse would agree to play Bart. Golf. Alone. With no one to protect him or keep the game square.

The Taj Mahal poker room got together a softball team that summer for a town league, some dealers and floor people and players. Mike Luma was there. And so was Bart Stone. On the team. Luma told me about one game they played down at the Brigantine field. It was one-pitch softball, where you get one good slow pitch to swing at, one swing. And Bart got up there in his all black, and looking mean and menacing with the bat, he laid down a bunt. Mike said it was so funny he fell on the ground and so did half the people there because you just don't do that in slow-pitch softball.

Bart isn't even close to being a regular guy. I do hear some funny testimonials, though. Old Man Sam says to me, "Nooo, you just gotta get to know him. . . ." And he tells me about when he and Bart went to the racetrack and Bart told funny stories about Tijuana and talked Spanish to some guys at the next table over and bought drinks for the whole bunch.

Of course, Old Man Sam's a little bit special himself. For me, he'll always live on as an Omaha player. I'll remember him perched on the edge of his chair over the table, taking one of those long pauses while he stares, first at the four cards in his hand, then at the cards on the table.

"On you, Sam . . ."

"I'm thinking . . ." His right fingers pick at the cards he's holding in his left hand. "Look at this goddamn shit." He tilts the cards so I can see them. I'm out of the hand. I lean my head over and cluck sympathetically.

"Mmm . . . tsk . . . That's raw, man." Actually, since

I'm sitting next to him I've already seen his hand. Old Man Sam doesn't have the best eyesight, so he's always holding his cards way up high to get a better look at them. But I never look unless I'm out of the hand already. Anyway, I know he's gonna call.

Old Man Sam is one of the most standup and straight-out guys I've ever met, but poker is poker. Or should I say, business is business. Anyway, Sam knows the score. Like he says, "Hey, man, I been a hussler all my life." Deep Philly accent. And he can size a guy up in three seconds flat, and then sum it up with one line that breaks up everyone within earshot because of its ring of sincerity. "That man? He ain't no hussler. That man's a turkey!"

Or when some chump at the table makes a really bad play, I mean a stinker, and everyone's pretending they didn't see, looking up in the air, praying the guy won't leave and he'll do it again and Sam says, "Man, what are you doing? I mean you got the right to do what you want with your own money, but you're just giving it away! Pretty soon you'll be out on Atlantic Avenue." But remember, Old Man Sam ain't there for the money. He's already got his. And then later, after the chump has left, Sam grabs my arm and says, "I know that man twenty-five years. He did me a big favor one time. I bring him a suitcase with eight hundred thousand in it and ask him to hold it for me."

"For what?"

"Business . . ." That's all he says. I try to make a quick mental list of acquaintances that I would trust to hold eight hundred grand for me.

Old Man Sam loves Bart. Old bored rich people always love him. Bart's like a second childhood, he's like being on the inside of a Western movie. Sam thinks he knows it all and has seen it all and has hustled so many of 'em for so long that he figures he can lie down with the lions and not get any fleas, or at least not get bit when they get hungry. Man, stuff just doesn't happen like that. Why? Because if you want to know Bart, you gotta pay. Pure and simple.

You see, because I know that Bart Stone doesn't have a regular life. It's someone else, and he's someone else, and I remember one time sitting in the Taj poker room and we wanted to get in touch with Bart, who was up in his room, and DB says, "He ain't staying under Bart Stone, that ain't his real name." And that kind of hit it home for me. That, and when I saw Bart in the car park.

Now it's just like a dream. It's like a dream because there were no witnesses. I was kind of in a fog from playing twelve hours of poker, and I'm waiting for my car in the Taj Mahal valet area. It's beautiful out, like nine in the morning and sunny and now I really need my sunglasses as I sit on a bench outside next to the big glass revolving door with a slight chill. Fresh air. Wrap my seventies sport coat closer around me.

Bart comes striding out the front door and walks through the valet area, a few cars lined up just to the side of the door, special parking places for VIPs and people with Lexuses and Lamborghinis that tip the guy a twenty spot so they can keep the car right there in front. Bart walks over to a car on the end. It's a white Lincoln Town Car. I've never seen Bart's car before, so I saunter over. Bart's on his knees at the rear tire, cursing like hell. "Motherfucker! Fuckin' cocksucking mother-fucker!" I get over there and it's a beautiful car, big and white and spanking shiny clean and the left rear tire is slashed. All the tires are slashed. Bart is white livid and he's just glaring, and I say, "Holy shit, Bart!" And then the valet comes driving up in my maroon Taurus and I drive home and think, a random act of vandalism and it's better not to leave your car out front. But man, that wasn't no random act of violence. All the guys Bart's robbed and stiffed and pissed off?

A couple months later a bunch of us are sitting around a poker table and everybody's in a good mood, even Bart, and I'm like, "Hey, Bart, remember that time we're outside and some guy slashed your tires?"

And he looks right at me and says in a dead calm voice, "I got no idea what you're talking about, Mickey." And I don't say anything more and neither does Bart, and y'know I'm sitting there and asking myself if it really happened. I mean that's how good he is.

EVEN THOUGH BART strikes most people as crazy, just plain nuts, I always think of him as smart. Devious, amoral, sly, yes, but most of all real goddamn intelligent. One day Bart is in Bart Stone mode, giving us all the Let's gamble hiiiir, boys.

I say to him, "Bart, these guys might all think you're stupid, but it wouldn't surprise me if you have a goddamn Ph.D.!"

He thinks that is so funny—I mean he really laughs—and

for months after, every once in a while Bart says to me in that dry rasp, "So what you say, Mickey. It wouldn't surprise you if I have a Ph.D.?"

And I say, "That's right, Bart, you might be a doctor or something." And there he goes laughing again, his own private joke. That motherfucker knows how smart he is.

Bart gives me shit about my outfits, my Salvation Army outfits. One of my favorite ensembles is a bright brown and white striped jacket with yellow pants. Real ugly jacket. Bart spots me walk into the room one day and says, "I'll give you five hundred dollars for that jacket."

"This jacket? Not a chance, Bart. You can't get these kind of clothes just anywhere, you know." I'd bought it for $2.80. Green-tag special at the shop on the Black Horse Pike.

"All right, eight hundred, but that's my final offer."

"Sorry, Bart, this jacket's worth a lot more than that."

All this witnessed by, and to the amusement of, all the players and live ones in the big game section of the Taj. It's like a little vaudeville act we put on for everybody to hide the fact that we're really only thinking of how to get some money out of the monkeys. Of course, to Bart, I am one of the monkeys.

He does make attempts to be friendly, sometimes. One day I'm sitting across the table from him looking really raggedy. I'm wearing an oversized light blue Naugahyde sport coat and I've got a blue felt hat and sunglasses and uncombed hair over my shoulders and Bart says in that Darth Vader voice, "Mickey, you know those guys that stand out there on the boardwalk holding out their little cups? Well, Mickey, let me know if you ever need money. Because I'm gonna set you up out there and, Mickey, I'll buy the cup!" And then he laughs his head off. "Mickey, I'll buy the cup!"

Bart laughed a lot about that cup. Some days we'd both be in a good mood and he'd start in about that cup and then we'd both sit there and laugh our heads off, one time Bart even reaching over to give me a high five.

He told that idea to everyone, and he'd always end it by saying to me, "Mickey, don't worry about nothin', because I'm gonna buy the cup." I never really minded. Hell, I'm wearing those clothes to get some attention. I like attention. This is when Bart is acting kinda friendly toward me. It's almost his friendliest.

THE SECOND FOXWOODS tournament promised to make the first look like a coffee klatsch. It's December of '93 and by this time Foxwoods has opened their hotel, special room rates are available to poker players for about half price. All the big game players are still hanging out in the relatively new poker rooms of Atlantic City, but they are planning on transporting themselves up to Foxwoods for tournament time. Almost everyone, that is. I have just returned from California where I got pulverized in the 40-80 Hold'em and don't much like the thought of squaring off with the best players in the world at astronomical limits. Or at least my bankroll is advising heavily against it. I don't generally fare well in tournaments either. Play is radically different between tournaments and ring games. So I stay in Atlantic City, a mere six-hour drive from the temporary poker center of the world.

But I keep up with the happenings, the gossip up there, through people who are going back and forth, or have partners in Connecticut. Like Isaac from New York City who is down to play Stud for a few days but has been up at Foxwoods last weekend. He says they are playing real high, 150-300 Hold'em, and Jimmy and Grouse and Fresca Kid and Crazy Roger and John Smiley are in the game and Autism and Phil Helmuth and they are playing high Stud and Pot-Limit. Then I hear from Tofu Trina who talked to Fresca Kid up there that John Smiley is getting all the money and I say, "But I thought he was broke?" I mean the last I saw him was in July, all in in the Hold'em game and strung out on Sambuca. Apparently he arrived in Foxwoods with two hundred bucks in his pocket, and knowing John he ain't looked back yet. Tofu Trina says he is playing everyone head up, taking on all comers.

I can picture John sitting at a table with two cushions under his ample butt and one behind his back to make his cards and chips easier to grab. So there he is, dwarfed by mountains of chips, with maybe two or three other guys at the table. But there is no question that John's in the driver's seat. When he's on a rush, when he's stroking those cards, John is something to watch. Playing, raising just about every hand, no hesitations, just bet or raise or sometimes fold but never at the wrong time and mostly the hands end with John turning over something goofy like a jack-six for two pair to win the pot. Or his opponent folds and concedes John the pot to which he merely nods, says Mmhmm like he expected it, and then peeks at his cards one more time before mucking them face down. As often as not John's on complete air, but only rarely does he let someone know when they've been bluffed. Usually they're busy calling him already. John never gets embarrassed about being caught bluffing. Sometimes he just says "Uh-oh."

John Smiley, who went from zero to having a quarter of a million in the eighties and then smoked it away. John, who arrived in Connecticut for the second Foxwoods tournament in December '93 with two hundred dollars in his pocket. Two weeks later he arrived in Atlantic City. I went up to his room in the Taj Mahal and he opened up a dresser drawer and in there among the dirty socks and T-shirts was sixty thousand dollars strewn about like Monopoly money.

To know John is to want to root for him. Maybe that only sounds strange if you play a lot of poker. After a while you just stop rooting for other people to win. I mean I still might say to Sportscar Bernie, Good luck, or, I'm glad to hear you been running good, or, Tsk-tsk sympathetically when he weaves over to wherever I'm sitting and gets really up in my face with his alcohol breath and tells me bad beat stories and how unlucky he is and what a dumb motherfucker every other person in the poker room is. But I'm not really rooting for him.

John's different. John's there and he doesn't care about himself. He's the only guy who doesn't care about whether he's up or down, unless he's gambling with someone else's money. When he has money he puts everyone in action.

After he won the sixty thousand he went out one day in AC and went to a mall and got himself a bunch of new clothes and he said it's the first time he bought new clothes in like six or seven years. And I remember he got a cotton sweater, mostly brown but with orange and purple colored patches on it like Lou Carnesecca's, and he wore that every moment I saw him for the next week. He really liked that sweater.

WHEN THE FOXWOODS tournament ended, the big game didn't end, it just moved southward to the Taj Mahal. And sometime in those days between the tournament and Christmas, when John Smiley came down to Atlantic City freshly on top of a gargantuan run, he and Bart Stone went out eating and drinking a few times, buddying together. John knew Bart Stone was bad, but he didn't know that Bart was pure evil.

Late one night John is sleeping in his room and Bart calls him and says he's got a guy wants to play gin and does John want to go partners against this guy, like they discussed one night when they were drinking, and Bart and this guy will come up to play in John's room? Bart, by the way, has a reputation as a great gin player. John doesn't. Of course John, sleepy and just himself, says okay.

A knock on the door five minutes later and Bart comes in followed by a guy John doesn't know, maybe he thinks he's seen the guy playing 10-20, maybe chumps all look alike at two in the morning. John clears his stuff off the table and Bart says they'll start with five thousand each and pulls out five and then the guy takes out a massive stack of hundreds from his pocket. John thinks that's kind of weird, but whatever. Bart says they'll play for two hundred a game—double for gin—and John says, "Fine, guys, but I'm real tired and I'm going to sleep." So John gives Bart five thousand out of the dresser drawer and then goes over to the bed to sleep.

And I can see the scene now as it happened. The Taj Mahal has these mini-suites, which is actually their way of saying small room with no windows but a couch and table and chairs and dresser and TV. The couch unfolds into a bed and is toward the rear of the room, and the table and chairs are at the front near the door that goes to the bathroom. So there's John Smiley, lying in bed trying to get some sleep after having played poker for twenty hours and having run two hundred dollars into sixty thousand in two weeks and wearing a T-shirt and shorts with his potbelly and his glasses on the night table next to the bed without which he can't even tell if you're holding up four fingers or five in front of his face. And not three feet from his head Bart and this no name sit across a table from each other, each with a massive stack of hundred-dollar bills in front of them, playing gin rummy. Bart, as always, dressed in all black, black hat, black leather coat, tall, thin, mean, talking in his hoarse voice, motherfucker this and motherfucker that, chain-smoking his Pall Mall cigarettes, trying to get John's attention into the game. And John couldn't care less, unsuspecting, believing people are essentially good at heart, and above all just dog goddamn tired and not caring at all about the five dimes he just gave to Bart.

The other fellow sitting across the table from Bart, the chump. Fifty-something and nondescript, his clothes are neither new nor expensive nor clean, and he looks kind of like a broken-down gambler or horse player who is dead broke and not the sort to pull a stack of money out so high you can only guess how much is there. And not even rubber-banded or wrappered into five-thousand-dollar or thousand-dollar or ten-dime piles, just there and loose, which is (coincidentally) how Bart carries his money when he has a lot of it to show he is a motherfucker and just don't care and let's gamble higher, boys, and get this game out of the dirt!

So there they are, the three of them in John's room and every time Bart loses a hand he slams the cards down on the table and hisses "Motherfucker" and jerks his legs and jumps up and stalks around the room and slams back into his chair and hisses "Deal!" And poor John has to open one eye that he can't see out of anyway and wish that they'd just finish and leave so he could get a little sleep.

They play for a while, trade a few games between them, and then Bart loses four or five in a row and the heat from his anger and the negative energy and motherfuckers coming from him are so strong you think maybe the carpet will catch fire or the roof will fall in or thank God he doesn't have a gun or he'll kill us all or he might anyway.

Now Bart comes over to John and starts whispering "This lucky motherfucker" and "This cocksucker" and "Come watch" and pestering and so John does the last thing in the world he wants to do, which is get up, fumble for his glasses, yawn, put them on, wait for the world to come into focus, and sit on the edge of the bed, behind Bart, and watch Bart play this guy gin with money that is half John's and half Bart's, from a pile of hundreds that's still pretty hefty but not as tall as the ten thousand dollars that they started with or the mountain of money across the table.

Bart plays a few hands with John watching. Now John doesn't know anything about gin, but John's been around gambling for a long time and he knows that there is a lot of

skill to gin and a good player will eventually beat a bad
player, or I'm assuming he knows that. But Bart definitely has
played gin and everybody knows that—he's got a gin reputation that precedes him. John's got card sense and he knows
don't throw cards which are too live and he might know some
more but I sure don't. Maybe he saw Bart make a play that he
wouldn't have done or maybe he didn't or maybe he just
didn't really care and was wondering when he could go back
to bed and is Bart really his buddy. I mean they'd been out
eating, drinking, and laughing a few times together and why
is Bart doing him this favor of letting him in on the action if
he has his own money and thinks he can beat the guy himself?

But all these thoughts more likely came later, much later,
like after a long sleep and a shower and room service, when
he is laying in bed going over the events detail by detail, and
not when he's been up for a day and a half playing poker and
hasn't really been outside a casino for over two weeks with not
much sleep and his mind is numb in that casino vacant-look
zombie-like state where nothing is real except for the action
and there's no beginning or end, just how much am I up or
how much I'm down. But maybe a tiny little thought, a seed,
is planted somewhere at the back of his brain. No more than a
feeling, but there and growing.

Meanwhile, Bart is rolling ahead full steam in full character and every time he takes a card he snatches it, throwing
discards down with vehement force, shaking the table with
convulsive jerks from his knees, at the end of every losing
hand slamming the table hard with his fist and a resounding
"Motherfucker" in that dry voice that sounds like someone's
death rattle.

Then Bart loses three hands in a row, getting ginned on the last one, and he throws down the cards, hurls four hundred dollars at the chump, kicks up from the chair while saying "Motherfucking cocksucker whore," turns around, takes one step so his back is to both John and the chump, takes a deep drag of his Pall Mall, is absolutely still as if looking for guidance for five long seconds, during which no one moves or does anything but stare at Bart, and then he turns around and points toward his chair, looks at John and rasps, "You play!"

John stares at Bart in the same uncomprehending zombie gaze that he's been following the proceedings with up to this point. He turns his head, his eyes following the line formed by Bart's still outstretched arm and finger toward the empty chair and beyond that the table with on it from front to back: an ashtray overflowing with a mountain of powerfully ground-out cigarettes and a mussed pile of hundred-dollar bills representing John and Bart's money, behind that the cards scattered all about the table—some up some down from the end of the last hand—and at the back of the table the bigger pile of hundreds representing the chump's money, and then beyond that John looks up a bit and sees the chump, immobile, very quiet, tense, and staring intently at John . . . staring at John.

Automatically, John makes to move toward the chair, but when he looks up again and sees the chump's face, boom! That teeny tiny thing gnawing at the back of his brain explodes and slams into the front of his head, jolts him awake, doubles his heartbeat, and widens his eyes. Something feels wrong. Something feels very wrong.

And now I see the whole thing quite clearly. John does too,

but at the time it's hard to know whether he saw the whole play laid bare like a chess player who suddenly sees the jaws of the trap that will inevitably spring shut seven moves ahead if care is not taken, or whether he just felt that something was wrong without putting a finger exactly on it and that it was time to cut loose. And like a lot of things in the gambling world, reality is illusory. Things may or may not be happening and depending on your point of view everybody is on a con and there are neither good guys nor bad guys. But I'll always pull for guys like John Smiley.

John gets up from the bed and sits in the chair that Bart has just vacated. He picks up the pile of hundreds in front of him and begins to count them slowly, laying them back down one by one onto the table—forty-eight hundred dollars. Now he picks up the pile and begins to count them again, this time a little bit faster. Nobody speaks. Bart and the chump are motionless, eyes only on John and the money he is counting. This time he stops at twenty-four. Now the money is in two piles. One he leaves on the table. He folds the remaining money and clenches it tightly in his left hand. Now John turns and says to Bart, his voice tired but firm, "I'm done. This is your money." He points to the pile on the table. "I'm tired and I want to go to sleep. If you still want to play him you'll have to go someplace else."

WHEN JOHN SMILEY tells me the story a few days later there are a few things that I don't completely understand. It's morning, I just finished playing all night—I won—and John has moved out of his mini-suite and brought Luma and me upstairs to check out the deluxe suite that he has somehow managed to finagle for the regular room rate.

So there we are, spread out on a big L-shaped couch and looking at the room service menu while John is telling the story now with hindsight, pointing out all the fishy parts. John's never seen the chump in the big poker game. Then there's all the money he pulled out that was organized in a Bart-type bankroll, the fact that he looked like a broke, and it looks like he's left town. And why would Bart want to give up half his action if he thought he could beat the guy himself? And why did Bart want John to play the guy with their money? When Bart knew that John didn't know a thing about gin, he insisted that John watch him, tried to get John involved in the action.

I've always considered Bart to be evil incarnate. So I am more than willing to agree with John that Bart cheated John out of his money by teaming up with the chump against him. But there are still a few points that don't make sense to me. Why had Bart insisted that John watch when John was perfectly happy just to sleep and find out how his five thousand dollars ended up later? Why did Bart tell John to play when he was perfectly capable of sitting there and losing the money himself?

Only two years later, on a beach far away from any poker game, when the hugeness of Bart slams me and all the pieces fit together like genius, does it become clear to me. Bart wasn't after John's five thousand dollars. His prize was much bigger. He knew about the sixty dimes that John had in that dresser drawer not five feet behind his head, and that was the only goal worthy of this con. Bart don't operate for small potatoes. Bart knows that John's not gonna want to go deeper than five thousand when he's not involved in the game and not playing himself. But if John gets involved in the game, if he agrees to play a few hands, starts trying to get even and gets in a deeper hole and then goes for just a few thousand more to try and get his money back, and then gets into the full gambling mode and heart pumping and chain smoking and on tilt and thinking about nothing but gotta get even gotta get even gotta get even. But there's no way he can get even because John can't play gin and this guy is a ringer and hell, he's got nothing to lose anyway because this chump is just some broke who happens to be a good gin player but doesn't have any money and it's all Bart's money anyway. And I'd just like to know what kind of cut Bart's gonna give the guy after, just to have a laugh.

John is pissed off, but the fact is that he's got a bankroll when he was broke three weeks ago and he hasn't been home yet and he says, "Yeah, the games are gonna be good here. I'm gonna get a ride home with Howie, and come back out here in a few weeks when I'm ready to stay a longer time. Right now I want to just sit back and see what this means."

And when we're at the Chinese restaurant on his comp, me

and John and Jimmy, and I say to John, "Now you got enough money so you don't have to go broke anymore," he says, "Yeah, right," but it's completely empty, a flat toneless phrase that just goes bong.

I GUESS JOHN must have got all the shit when he was in Ohio. Maybe along with a different attitude. I shouldn't be bitter—I mean, I survived. New Year's Eve, 1993. John is home in Ohio, enjoying his cash windfall from the Foxwoods tournament, but I'm in Atlantic City, where New Year's Eve is one of the busiest nights of the year. And the Taj Mahal is the place to be.

As the clock turns twelve I'm sitting in a packed 50-100 game. I think I know everyone in the game. It's New Year's Eve, yet almost all the players are here alone. I'm wearing my blue and black shiny checkered disco pants with a blue fake velvet shirt and an antique navy-blue policeman-style blazer. I just picked up the outfit where else but at the Salvation Army for about four dollars. It's drawing some stares. But it's a holiday and everyone's in a party mood and to the gills and the Taj is full of tuxes and glittering party dresses and people-watching is just the thing to do. Jimmy's sitting at the table. We're still just acquaintances right now, but we've been playing together a lot lately.

Jimmy had a miserable trip up at the Foxwoods tournament. He set a personal loss record in one session of 150-300

Hold'em. During those two weeks Jimmy became friendly with John Smiley through bullshitting and playing together, and when Jimmy ran a little short of on-hand cash John willingly lent him five or ten dimes until they both came down to Atlantic City. Things like that always seem to come back to you. Like garlic.

Vinnie the Greek is in the game, too. He always looks dapper. Jimmy roomed with him up at Foxwoods for the tournament and told me that Vinnie had a different pair of shoes for every day. The cocktail waitresses are all circulating with trays of champagne and as it nears midnight the noise level rises and rises, and the action slows down.

At midnight Vinnie the Greek, always the gentleman, stands up and goes around the table wishing Happy New Year in his heavily accented English, and offering everyone his large hand with the gold rings and the big gold bracelet that says Vince on the thick wrist just below his huge hairy forearms.

My friend Emily is in town from Vermont and three of her girlfriends are up from Washington, so for the night I'm actually leading a whole party around. So why play poker except that Emily wants to see me play and so I'm flashing money and feeling like a big man and really the center of the party because all the poker players want to meet these beautiful women. Me, not known around the poker circles as a ladies' man and for good reason 'cause I'm not. And all the dealers and floor people that I know and everyone's saying, Hi, Mickey, and, Happy New Year, and shaking hands and after midnight just about everyone plays the first hand so you can say that you won the first pot of the year and set precedent for the next twelve months.

I don't play very long that night. It's more a time for partying and reflection than moneymaking and I'd been hitting 'em pretty well lately. We're all standing on the mezzanine—me, Emily, and her three friends—where you can look over the balcony down to the crowded lobby below and watch the people. There's an obese man standing in the center of a crowd wearing a tailored black suit with a white silk scarf and reptile-skin shoes.

None of the girls have ever been in a casino before, and amid the lights, bells, people, money, chips, sequins, champagne, and the lightning momentum of the pulsating casino—like a gambling techno beat—they think it's all just completely crazy and suddenly I have this feeling like of course it's crazy, wacky, what the hell is going on and how can things ever be the status quo here unless you're really unbalanced? Maybe that's why I'm beginning to get inside of these kooky clothes. To match the million-dollar chandelier hanging over my head. It's the size of a Volkswagen bus, made out of gold and silver shiny and lights and is so unbelievably ostentatious and tacky that half the people seeing it for the first time say, Oh wow, and the other half say, No fucking way.

I'm standing here and thinking now it's almost three years and I'm still here, still in action, three years since I've had a job, a regular job. When I was broke living in New Orleans and Cato came down for Mardi Gras and staked me to seven hundred bucks in a 20-40 game way out in the bayou of Louisiana in an abandoned warehouse and when you knocked on the door the guy who opened the sliding panel for the peephole had a loaded shotgun. Seven hundred bucks that he knew I couldn't pay back and it wasn't like he was so flush himself, and I won twenty-four hundred dollars in the game and went to Vegas four days later and to California and back to Vegas and Connecticut and AC and now here I am standing looking back and thinking that almost everyone I knew along the way went broke or went on drugs or quit poker or dropped way down or got a job and here I am still going up, playing higher, making money. And I'm reminded of a short story by Stephen King called "The Long Walk," where a group of people march on a long walk and if you stop you get shot. They keep on walking until only one person is left. Well, it's an interesting idea and an exciting story but when at the end the narrator is the only one alive, the only person still walking, you're wondering, why him? What makes this guy so special? Because in the story he appears neither stronger nor smarter nor healthier than anyone else, and that's how I feel right now. I'm doing something that 99.99 percent of all attempts at fail, and after three years I'm still here. Why me? All around me people are desperate, going broke, trying to borrow a little here, parlay there, rob this guy, get someone in the middle and burn, rape, and pillage. Let's gamble, boys.

IV

BONKERS
MONSTER

IT WAS A few weeks after the Foxwoods tournament, January 1994, and John Smiley came riding into Atlantic City in a brand-new red sports car that he bought—cash—with some of the score he'd just made in Foxwoods. He only brought five thousand dollars cash with him because he didn't trust himself not to get stupid and blow his whole load in one night, and he figured he could always borrow some cash from me and Jimmy. He was right on both counts. Jimmy is still staying in a room at the Taj, where he's been for the better part of six months. John stayed with him and Jimmy started getting nervous pretty fast about whether or not the maids would find John's cocaine all over the room. He left it in a little pile on the room table under a magazine where it was easy for him to make quick cuts into lines. And then there was that industrial-size bag of pot in the dresser drawer.

The day after John Smiley arrived was the first night I ever lost ten grand. A 100-200 Stud game and Jimmy had 25 percent of me. I called John on the house phone and said, "Please can I have one joint? Tell Jimmy we just lost ten thousand." John thought I meant Jimmy's end was ten thousand, which would have meant that I lost forty dimes. That made me laugh a little, but mostly I just felt numb. Jimmy took it pretty well. He's always a cool rider. Then I went home and smoked the joint and went for a long walk on the beach and talked to the pigeons and asked myself what the hell was going on (no answer), mentally regrouped, climbed back on the horse, ate a big meal, and went to sleep.

Part of the reason things were weird was because of all the taking pieces and everything. I mean it's hard enough keeping your own shit together. It's not that it's impossible to make money at poker in the long run. It's just that you'd be better off packing up your stuff and going to Alaska to dig for gold.

You can say what you like. I maintain winning poker is the changing of chaos to order, of always perceiving order. But everything associated with casinos and their effect on people has to do with the loss of order, perceptions of chaos—no clocks, no windows, free alcohol, bright lights, bells. It's the same with gambling, the drug produces chaos—rapid heartbeat, adrenaline pumping, things moving fast, chips instead of money, in, out, bad judgment. And it's tough keeping yourself under tight control night after night, which is why in the gambling world there's an entire vocabulary for losing control. Tilt. Going off, losing your shit, steaming, hot, the bonkers monster.

Like playing 100-200 the three-way game and it's like 10 A.M. and we've been playing all night and at like four in the

morning we switched tables because they had to clean. The
game has been a hummer all night and Jimmy's in it and
John Smiley is in it and I'm in it, and Jimmy and I are
swapping thirds with each other and I'm lending John money.
I started the night out ahead but now I'm stuck fifteen
dimes—or really only ten because Jimmy's out the other five,
and poor Jimmy, because he's losing too. I played good most
of the night but now I've just lost it and I know I must be
playing real bad because everyone's kind of quiet to me and
some live ones quit and now I'm kinda the main action in the
game. Jimmy's not saying anything. He's sure got class, or
maybe he's just stupid, but he's looking at me with questioning eyes when I play a hopeless Stud hand down to the end.
No, not questioning, more like a long, sorry, and sorrowful
look like yes, you and me we're both suffering. Maybe I'm
imagining the whole thing. I mean I can barely make out his
eyes anyway through his dark glasses.

At one point, what with giving John a few thousand and
being stuck fifteen myself, I plumb haven't got any money
left except for a scattering in my casino box. So I walk over to
get at it at the cage, which is only about fifteen feet away, but
they're doing some sort of counting procedure or some shit
and the cage is closed. They say it's gonna be closed for an
hour or so. And I'm standing there trying to stay calm wearing a 1930s maroon pinstripe three-piece gangster suit that
looked real wild and crazy and made a big hit in the poker
room when I came gallivanting in about fourteen or fifteen
hours before. Now it's wrinkled and smelly and hot and not
real comfortable and I'm really tired and stuck ten dimes and
John owes me five and Jimmy will owe me and I can't get any
money to gamble with because the cage is closed. And I don't

want to stand there not playing because if I stand there then I have to think, and if I think all I can think about is how there was one time in the early part of the night when I was actually ahead a few thousand and now I'm playing bad, real bad, and just giving money away and I'm actually the live one now because Floyd got even and quit and so did Iberville Tom and there ain't nobody playing real bad now. It's just Wiggy the cheater and Brock the fuckin' angle shooter, toothpick or non-filtered Camels staring at you, analyzing you, always Whadid you have there, Mick? Two pair? Always shooting fuckin' angles, and then there's Jimmy playing good and John who seems to have settled way down the last couple of hours and yes, I guess he's actually playing all right, and what the hell am I doing here except gotta get even get even get even gotta just get a little lucky and get even and . . . Yeah, fat chance.

Now Gerry the shift manager comes over—she's just getting on shift—and she pats me on the back and says, "Hey, Mickey, nice suit!" Bright, cheery, she's really sweet and just trying to be nice but I'm too far gone and tired and stuck and I'm like, I gotta get in my box, and I try to explain to her that it's a hurry and an emergency. I mean I'm stuck so bad I don't even want to go to the bathroom much less stand here in front of the cage and miss a few hands and she says she'll see what she can do and gives me a buffet comp while I'm standing there. And I'm thinking, Great, in one night I've lost and loaned and whatevered over twenty thousand bucks, which is like half of all my assets and most of the cash, and I can get a free meal at the coffee shop—a bagel and a cup of grease.

But that's how unreal those things go and now John gets up and walks over. Maybe he senses I'm way out, and he says, "Look, Mickey, I'll cash out and give you all the chips I got so

you can play until you can get your money. But look, the
game's not so good anymore and you've been playing a long
time and you're really not playing so well now, so why don't
you go get a little sleep."

And you know, nobody will actually tell you you're playing
bad, gently, and it's really what I need to hear. Because I'm
not gonna tell it to myself and all of the sudden I feel really
absurd because I been up all night and besides Jimmy I don't
see anyone who's been here that long. It's all bright and
cheery midmorning faces just coming in to work or gamble
and lots of, "Hey, what's up, Mickey," and "Where'd you get
the suit?" And I'm standing at the cage with dark glasses, a
straw hat, a three-piece suit, I'm offended by my own smell
and I'm clutching a piece of paper that says I'm entitled to a
free buffet at the Bombay Cafe.

John's standing there across from me saying, "All right, I'll
see you later, and I'll get that check sent, and there'll be a
good game later and I really appreciate you lending me." And
like the fact that somehow I'm not in direct possession of
twenty-five thousand dollars cash that I had yesterday and all
I have to show for it is the words from two gamblers amount-
ing to about twelve thousand dollars and a ten-dollar coupon
for breakfast and a big fog in my head, that this is the most
natural thing in the world and let's regroup and worry about
it later. And John, who's been rich and broke and on top and
burned out so many times and round and round, on these
matters he knows what he's talking about. So I nod my head
and slowly walk out of the poker room and get a paper and go
home and, too tired to sleep, I turn on the TV, light a joint,
and stare blankly at the crossword puzzle. Here come the
poker hallucinations.

IT'S STILL DARK when I wake up—no, not dark—just dark gray. I go straight into the poker room. Don't pass go, don't collect two hundred dollars. It's not even seven yet and I didn't have much of a sleep, just jumped awake out of a dream and thought, What's happening in the poker room? Time to try and get some money back, time to keep an eye on the guy who I lent five dimes to, the guy I got 10 percent of.

The worst part is from my door down the steps to my car. No winter jacket, not for the poker room. Just jeans, velour shirt, orange plaid sport coat, cap, and sunglasses, and it's freezin' fuckin' cold as I'm hopping around trying to get my door open—frozen stuck. And then my fingers, numb on the steering wheel or pressed up against the vent during most of the drive before the heat gets working. And then about three minutes before I get to the Taj Mahal I'm comfortably warm and one minute later I got the heat off and the window open and cold is the last thing on my mind as I slip into the almost empty valet area. I get out, get my ticket, go through the revolving door, and turn to my right to walk into the poker room.

As I turn toward the high-limit section I see a black hat on a man, long and lean. Bart, unmistakable even with his back to me. As I get closer, I see John. He's sitting back in his chair watching the dealer shuffle. From about twenty feet away I can't tell if John has his eyes closed or not. I guess it doesn't matter—zombie stare is zombie stare. He's not moving.

I get up to the table. There's two cigarettes burning in John Smiley's ashtray. DB sees me coming. He has a piece of Bart. He's sitting in the two seat next to Bart, sweating him. Bart's in the five seat just opposite the dealer and John's in the eight seat, facing DB.

"Hey, Mickey, your man needs some help over here!"

"What's up, DB? How is it, Bart?"

"Mickey." That's all Bart says. And he nods his head one time. Ain't no reason for him to ever wear sunglasses. His eyes just look all mean all the time.

"How's it going, John?"

"Well, I'm losing . . ." That I could tell. Look at all the chips that Bart's got.

"What uh . . . What are you guys playing?" It's everyone has gotta draw the line somewhere. Actually, a lot of people manage to go through life without having to draw a line at all, but if you play poker, if you gamble, if you do drugs, you better draw that line because sure enough you're gonna be slammed up against it often enough, and one step over—well, it's just over.

"Mind if I sit here, John?"

"No, it's fine."

I pull a chair over from the next table and sit on John's left, slightly behind him where I can see his cards when he lifts them up off the table. He doesn't take any pains to conceal them. Heads-up play is not a cramped undertaking. A waitress swings by and I order my usual insta-wake-up, black coffee and a grapefruit juice. She replaces John and Bart's ashtrays. Both are filled to overflowing.

Bart Stone and John Smiley are finally playing head up and I got a ringside seat. It's seven in the morning and there ain't no way I'm gonna miss this one because John's my hero and also because he owes me five thousand dollars and I got 10 percent of him. The poker room is really quite empty and besides me the only guy watching the game is Ken, the floorman, who's more interested in looking at my crossword puzzle.

Just another poker game, just another poker game. This one is three and six hundred and there's about fourteen thousand dollars in black hundred-dollar chips on the table and it's easy to see who's won the last big pot because right now Bart has all those black chips in front of him in three towering stacks. And Bart, Bart's just so tall and sits way up high and jerks all around and bends his head down and when he reaches down to make a raise he grabs so that he has more than twelve chips in one hand and then snakes his hand out around the stacks. "Raise!" The voice of death. And then thunk-thunk-thwept, three piles of four chips all in a row, twelve hundred dollars. Call and raise. Yeah, Bart's got all the chips in front of him.

For every cigarette that John smokes, there's another one that he absent-mindedly lights and leaves burning in the ashtray. Two mostly empty coffee cups on coffee-stained paper napkins are on the table next to the ashtray, and three packs of Marlboro Reds. One pack is empty and one is less than half full. John's shoes are off and his feet, clad in dirty white socks, are stretched out and propped up on an unused chair at the side of the table. They've been here awhile. John never even leans forward in his chair anymore except maybe to get the last card in a big pot. Craig, the dealer, is doing a good job of keeping the game moving, stacking both their bets and pushing the cards close in front of the players.

I watch them play for a while—three minutes and they've both completely bowled me over. Holy cow. They're playing so good. Neither player gives an inch. John has got nerves of . . . John hasn't got any nerves at all.

So Bart Stone and John Smiley are finally playing head up, 300-600 half and half. Half Stud and half Hold'em. Generally, Bart's game is Stud and John's is Hold'em. At least those are their MOs. But John once told me, "Everybody calls me a Hold'em player, but I don't care so much. When you get short-handed, poker is poker, one and the same."

They're playing Hold'em right now and John needs some help. His chips are shrinking. They go back and forth awhile, John trying to make some headway into Bart's pile. A big hand builds. John's got king-ten and the flop is ten eight four and John check raises Bart on the turn, but when an ace hits on the river John raps down his hand in disgust, he knows he's beat. Bart bets and turns over ace-eight . . . ace or eight was his only out.

"Lucky shit." That hand hurt John.

"You fucking cocksucker. Your mother's a fucking whore!"

"Just shut up about my mother, asshole."

Bart's head is down low near the table and he swings it up in a half circle so everything's moving and the words get hurled out of his mouth in that dry hiss, extra loud. "I said she's a fucking whore!"

Silence. John's hand goes white around the coffee cup and I swear he's gonna throw it at him. Bart's fuckin' there in his face and John, John is just so tense I don't know what the fuck is gonna happen. What a fuckin' asshole this Bart is. And his whole game is just to get John off his. And it's working.

Two hands later, John's all in. Bart doesn't waste any time. "You still playing?" You evil motherfucker, Bart.

John looks up at me. "Can I talk to you a second?"

We both walk two tables down and outside the glass door. Now we're in the hallway. Separated from Bart by a glass wall. Well, actually a long glass picture window, we can see in and they can see out. On my right side is Bart and the poker room. On my left side is the valet window. In front of me is John. He's hooked and he knows it. He ain't got time for much.

"So what's up, John?"

"Well, I'm losing."

"How uh . . . How do you think you're playing?"

"I don't know." John's fidgety. He's fidgeting his hands and shuffling his feet. And looking up and down and at me and at the guy passing us on his way to go to the bathroom.

Bart's back at the table, watching us, bullshitting with DB. Acting like he don't care or don't know, but he knows the whole score. Knows that right now I got the bullets and I'm the guy he's gonna get the money from. He's gonna try and win it from John, but he knows what the bulges mean in my front jeans' pockets, double barreled. Don't carry money around unless you expect that you might lose it. Not in a casino. Not around gamblers. Or be stupid like me and a million other guys.

John has already lost ten thousand, five from me and five from Jimmy. I had 10 percent of him, so he only owes me four.

"Look, Mickey, he's got me hooked ten and it's personal. I want to keep playing. I don't want you to do something you don't want to do and gosh, I mean you've been a real friend already. Yeah, it's just up to you. I mean, I want to play."

"So, hold it. How much you want? Ten more?"

"Yeah. I can either call my friend or I can drive home and get the money."

"Look, John, I mean if you say you got it, then you got it. I'm not really worried about getting paid back." Yeah, sure. "I don't really know what I should do. . . ." Famous last words.

"Look, you don't have to take a piece of me anymore. This is just personal. If you don't want to do it, it's no problem, I understand and I appreciate everything you've done for me. But I mean I got the money, y'know, I got thirty thousand sitting with my friend . . ."

"Yeah, pffhytt, I don't know, John, I mean, are you sure you want it? I don't want you to do anything that you're gonna regret. I mean you're my friend, and I don't know, y'know you might feel different about it later." Like when you're straight.

"Look, I just really want to beat that asshole bad."

Of course I gave him the ten thousand. I can't really say no to John. I just want him to win so bad, I want Bart to go down, I want to see Bart break. Like Bart breaks. "But look, John, you definitely have the money, right? And I need it back right away, no matter what happens."

Oh shit, oh shit.

We walk back in. John gets up to the table holding a five-thousand roll in each hand. One he tosses in front of Bart. The other he puts behind his piddly pile of chips, more like a scattering. Bart looks up. "How much is it?"

"It should be five," I say.

DB pipes in, "Here, give it to me. I'll count it." Bart hands him the roll and DB starts riffling through it.

"You want to change both of 'em?" Bart directs himself toward the other one. "Mickey, you count it." Like Bart knows, 100 percent for sure, that even when I'm getting robbed for my last few dollars by a fuckin' snake in the woods, I don't have what it takes to cheat on the count. He's right.

They start playing again, Stud. Then the new dealer comes in and John says, "It's Hold'em." And Bart moves up and down and hisses, "No more Hold'em! Stud."

"No, it's time for Hold'em."

"Fuck Hold'em. I ain't playing no more fuckin' Hold'em."

"We made a deal."

"Fuck the fuckin' deal!"

"Wow, you're not . . . tthh, you're not even worth talking to. . . . All right, deal Stud. I can't believe this."

Wow, Bart is a fuckin' evil guy. Now he's got John hooked and he's gonna squeeze him, take away Hold'em, make him grovel, drive him into the ground.

But John, John Smiley's playing hard, man. He plays so good, I'm boggled by what he does, what he knows during the hands. But Bart's right there, he's no fucking slouchy player, and he's getting the cards too, and he's grinding him, grinding him down.

Two floor people come over for the daily counting of the dealer's box. "I'm sorry, guys, but we're gonna have to stop the game for a few minutes."

John's got about six thousand in chips left. He says, "I'm going up to the room for a second. You wanna come?"

There's not much to say in the ride up to John and Jimmy's room. "Whhirrr" says the elevator in a high-pitched hum. It's one of the elevators on the end, and as it rises way above the casino we can see Atlantic City through the big glass wall.

John leads the way into the room. He walks straight to an open dresser drawer and pulls out a pair of socks, a Baggy of pot, and a pipe. He puts the socks back. I walk in past the bathroom, past the bed where Jimmy's asleep in a tangle of sheets and blankets, and across to the round table under a hanging lamp. I sit down on a chair with a shirt hanging on the arm.

"Here you go. I don't have any papers, but you can use this pipe."

"Yeah, it's fine, John." Jimmy sits up for about three noncomprehending seconds and falls back down. He's out. "Sorry, Jimmy. Oh, you been playing all night, huh?"

"Mmm . . ." he says and rolls over to the other side of the pillow.

John sits down at the table across from me. He lifts up a magazine and the cocaine is right there on the table and he cuts off a line and snorts some and I'm packing some pot into a pipe and Jimmy's motionless on the far bed and John starts talking fast and I have to tell you he don't sound good. He's saying, "Look. I'm finished. I just wanna get fifteen thousand down there so I can give five to Jimmy and ten to you and then just go home and owe you four and get my money. He's just outplaying me."

"Whoah. He's really fuckin' playing good right now, John. He just ain't giving nothing away."

"I wasn't exactly catching any cards either. But I mean I just can't seem to catch when I need it."

"Yeah, I know. It's unbelievable. He's such a fucking jerk!"

"I'm just sick of this whole thing," he says and he's snorting another line and he says, "Are you ready? I gotta get back down quick. Just take your time, let yourself out. I'll see you down there." And I say, "Play good, John," and he says, "Yeah," and he's out the door. And the door shuts behind him and it's silence, and then just the sound of me taking a big hit of pot. I breathe out and I look around and I'm like, shit! He owes me fourteen thousand dollars and he's doing cocaine and Bart is fuckin', I never seen such a cold-blooded evil guy and he's playing so good and he got John off his game and holy fuck! I hope he just gets lucky, what the hell am I doing? Oh, man, this is messed up. All right, so let's see . . . John owes me fourteen and I got about two in my Vegas account and five in Connecticut and four in Natwest and whoah! What if he doesn't send me the money? No, he's gonna pay me back. Just concentrate on yourself.

And Jimmy, a lost soul in the corner. He's just trying to stay in action—like me—like the rest of us. Grateful for small moments of sleep, no matter how fitful, when there's no up and no down and no one wants anything from you and life will remain suspended as long as you can stay in your dream world. Jimmy doesn't have to fight too hard to ignore me. He's been up too long and his body is just about broken from living six months inside this hotel room and the poker room. And when I think about John, about what I'm doing, it's just hell, man.

When I got downstairs, it was all over. I had a million billion hopes and dreams, but what I wanted more than anything was for John to go down there and beat that fucker. I don't care how lucky or skill or whatever and then John would win and the bad guy would lose and I would get my

money and John would be a new man and just like a goddamn fairy tale. I've given a guy like most of my money to
gamble with and I'm sitting in a casino hotel room stoned and
my best-case scenario is that the whole shebang has a fairy-
tale ending. And this is how I make my living.

I come into the poker room to find John alone at the table.
"Where's Bart?"

"I guess he quit. His chips were gone when I got down
here. Shit. All right, look . . . I just wanna get out of here."
I guess Bart knew John was finished. I guess he knew John
was just gonna try and pull a hit and run on him. I guess he
didn't give a fuck about anything but the money. I guess it
wasn't very personal with him. He ended up beating John
Smiley for fourteen thousand that night. John's finished. He
paid off what he could and left town the next day.

EVERYBODY KNOWS I'M lending John money and they
all think I'm crazy, stupid, and that John is a broke crack
addict who will never pay me back and think how much
money I have if I can lend John twenty thousand. But the
truth is, I didn't think I was really lending him the money.
Now I think that you're always lending them the money.
Whether it's holding it for five minutes, or can you just
lemme hold some money till my wire transfer comes, or my
friend gets here, or that guy pays me, or the bank opens, or I

go to my box but my sister-in-law has the key so tomorrow night, c'mon. It's always lending, if they don't have it there then it's lending, and it's all the same.

Crazy Roger takes me aside and says, "Mickey, I know it's none of my business except I like you and don't want to see something bad happen to you, and I just thought you should know that John don't have such a great reputation for paying people back. I talk to Iberville Tom a lot and he knows John from way back, and he won't lend him anymore, no more than two thousand. You do what you want with your own money, I'm just saying it ain't a particularly good spot, you know what I'm saying?"

And Brock calls me over where he's holding court as table captain in a 50-100 stud game. "How much you give Smiley?" he demands of me from behind his mirror sunglasses and drawing hard on his Camel straight. Like a fuckin' interrogator. Brock needs all the information, needs to know everybody's deal in the poker room so he can shoot all the angles. And maybe they all wanna understand it because I don't lend money, don't have a reputation for it. Say not much more than yes, and I guess it's a way to show that every leak, no matter how small, has the potential to break you.

You never know whether someone's good for the money. I mean you never know. John Smiley left town and he owed me fourteen thousand plus five thousand that I somehow got conned into giving Brock for the five thousand that John owed him. So John owed me nineteen thousand dollars, which I was kind of fine about until he left town and then I'm talking to people and they all say he's gonna stiff me and John says, check's in the mail. Sure enough, three days later three checks arrived in the mail for five thousand each—and they cleared.

John calls me at home and says, "If you're really in trouble I can get you the four thousand," and I just say, "No problem, John, give it to me when you get it and just try and get your shit sorted." Anyway, I'm more than happy for the fifteen thousand.

But you never know. There's this guy named Vic who appears in the high-limit games once every few weekends and he's a gentleman gambler and likes to gamble high and sometimes I see him busted on the rail and I always get on well with him and his wife who's super nice and always sits at an empty table nearby while he plays and gossips with everyone on the rail about her grandchildren.

So I've played 75-150 with Vic and 150-300 with him and one day I guess he's gone broke for the weekend, but I don't know his business—that's the whole point—and he comes up to me when I'm about to cash out one day and I got a whole lot of chips and he says, "Can I have a hundred bucks for a while?" and I say, "No, sorry." And he says okay and goes away but he's hurt and I feel bad about it, I mean a hundred bucks.

A few months later I'm in a poker room somewhere and Vic walks up to me and says, "Hey, Mickey, don't you know John Smiley pretty well?" And I say, "yeah," and he hands me two hundred dollars and says, "Could you give this back to him when you see him? I owed him this money." Now I just feel like an asshole. Now I feel like Bart.

It just goes to show you never know shit. But there are some people out there who think pride means something.

YOU CAN WANT the good guys to win, you can pray for it, you can believe in it. But the poker world eats them up and spits them out and says, success? As long as success involves money then that's the only thing it involves, and as long as it involves ethics then that's another thing. Go for the throat. And if you can't, then deal with your weakness. Change it into tilt, alcohol, drugs, blackjack, or whatever.

Like Jimmy, when I called him from Austria. I'd lost eighteen straight and seventy thousand and I'm cooling off in isolation and 20-40 in Vienna, and I catch Jimmy at home, miracle of miracles. He just got in from playing all night and I say, "How is it, Jimmy? How are the boys and the gang?"

And he says, "Well, poker couldn't be going better. I've been playing nonstop and the games have been real good and I won forty thousand for the month but . . ."

"Well, that's excellent, Jimmy!"

"Yeah. But I went to the pit . . ."

"Oh shit! Jimmy, what happened?"

"I don't know. I got real drunk and I blacked out and apparently I lost fifty thousand."

"Oh shit! Jimmy what are you gonna do?"

"Just get it back, I guess."

"Yo, man, stay out of the pit. I mean you just can't fuckin' go in there. . . ."

"Yeah, I know." And as I hang up the phone standing in a phone booth on a street corner in northern Vienna in the middle of fuckin' Europe, it's like there's no way out.

Eighteen times in a row. Eighteen sessions with negative results. Sixteen entries in my disintegrating poker ledger. Disaster. If you put all your stock in a philosophy, don't get upset if your world starts to shake when it starts talking malarkey.

Funny thing about losing eighteen times in a row is that most of what I remember is things I did when I wasn't playing poker. I guess that can't be saying much for my concentration. It all started up in Connecticut where I drove, ironically, to get a break, take stock away from the crazy action of the Taj Mahal where I had been hitting 'em pretty good. In between two marathon sessions where I almost lost all my money and ended up only losing a chunk, I shopped for underwear and shorts in the Norwich, Connecticut, Kmart because I went to Connecticut on a complete impulse without even going home to fetch clothes. I just left on a hunch, walking out of the Taj Mahal casino with rolls of money in my belt. I was so sure I had it together during a large-coffee middle-of-the-night ride up to Foxwoods, cruising up the highway thinking about how focused I was and how stuck they would all be when I burst in on them at six in the morning. Wrong hunch.

Yeah, but about the eighteen times in a row. I didn't start out trying to break any record. I guess maybe I finished trying to. I mean I remember distinctly one time in the Taj Mahal where I had been playing almost five hours and I was ahead like seventy-five bucks or something and I thought to quit and Morty advised me heavily to quit. It was the same night I had gotten my hair cut for the first time in two years and I'd lost about nine or ten in a row at this point and I just should have gone home and cursed the streak. But maybe I needed to see that doom doesn't have to have an end and just because the roulette ball has come up black fourteen times in a row, don't go betting on red again. Just walk away.

And maybe I learned the lesson vividly. Because that was the only end for that streak. Just walk away. Or go broke. Or run through the valley of the shadow of death because you get through the valley quicker that way. Or go home, lock your door, pace the floor, pace the house, flip the channel, grind marijuana stems, listen to every CD, go to the market and construct elaborate huge meals not to eat because everything makes you sick, mumble, talk out loud, put your palm to your forehead, cry out and groan, and want to go back into that poker room but be so scared to do it that in the end I just had to leave town, had to leave the country, in fear of what might happen with me in proximity to my money.

What do I remember. I remember sitting on my couch and staring at the TV and flipping through every one of the eighty channels twice and then walking into the kitchen and opening the refrigerator and then closing it and opening it again and closing it and walking into the den and looking at all the CDs and then putting one on and listening to one song and then looking at the crossword and then upstairs to the bedroom and back down to the living room and through the kitchen into the den to see what time it is on the TV again. And I think I can't go into the casino and I got to get out of town because I don't have anything to do except go into the casino. And all the while I'm replaying hands, replaying games, replaying losing sessions and decisions and finally getting so frustrated and driving on in to the casino with new promises and ever galloping toward that eighteen in a row.

I remember going into the casino for the last time and pledging not to play any higher than 30-60 and I already knew I was leaving town soon and there was no game but all of the sudden the millionaire asshole prince was in the room and wanted to play and people were locking up seats for 100-200 Stud quicker than you could say boo, and one of the floormen locked up a seat for me just to be nice. He knew I was running bad, hell, everybody knew, and I had the seat to the millionaire's left but it was a bad-luck seat and I got dealt right out of two thousand so painfully that I knew I had to go right then and not go back into the Taj Mahal poker room until something changed. Until something really changed.

I didn't come into Vienna with much cash, but I guess I hit 'em pretty good right from the start. And thank God, because I sure was at the end of my rope. I got into town on an off night, apparently most of the regulars were in Baden for a tournament and after getting completely ripped off by the cab driver, forty bucks for like a six-dollar fare, I showed up at the card room fresh with all my bags from Amsterdam, where it had taken me six days of sitting in coffee shops and aimlessly walking the streets to decide I should have another go at it. Every day I would smoke a massive joint and then go into an arcade in the center of town where they had a game where you could hold a big gun and shoot bad guy after bad guy on a movie screen. I killed about a million of them before I was ready to come out of catatonia.

I sat in the dining room just off the card room while waiting for my name to be called. All I had on me was a couple of traveler's checks, half of which I cashed. The biggest game going was a 50-100 schilling Stud game. About five- and ten-dollar limit. Pretty small, but what the hell do I care, my poker laurels are down to zero, and I just need to win in a game, any game.

About eight o'clock that evening, the floorman comes over to where I'm a little bored but enjoying being ahead almost a hundred dollars in a poker game since forever. "We have some players interested in starting up a higher-limit game this evening," he says. 500-1000 schilling Stud. Hello. Now there's a jump. A 50-100 dollar game out of nowhere. And I barely even have my feet wet yet. I look down at the eleven thousand schillings in front of me, and think about the remaining eight hundred U.S. dollars in my pocket. Not nearly enough. But fate's gotta spin.

There are only three other players to start the 500-1000 schilling Stud game. I've got eleven thousand schillings, and I guess I ain't gonna say no. I can't remember the particulars, all I know is that I held my own pretty good for most of the night, and then about four in the morning a crew-cut Dutchman named Hurst showed up looking unbelievably fresh and suggested we switch the game to Hold'em, which I was all for. By eleven I'm ahead about thirty thousand schillings in the game, almost three thousand dollars.

I remember how surprised I was by Hurst's play. I mean there I was spending all night thinking, Oh, my God, no one here has ever really played poker before. And then just as it turned to the wee hours and people couldn't be more oiled up, the machine shows up. And all I can tell you is that right from the start I could tell it wasn't such a great idea to be playing pots that Hurst was in. He'd had a good thing going in this town since poker had become legal only one year before, and I learned to expect him like clockwork at 4 A.M., just when everyone's wheels came off.

Vienna drifts into a blur after that first night. It was noon, I'd been in town for twenty-one hours and I didn't have a room yet. There were no hotels near the card room, which was in a working-class neighborhood, felt like the outskirts of town, but at least it had the good fortune to be located right next to a bus and streetcar line. I made it to the center of town toting both my bags into an English bookstore where the plan was find a guidebook about Vienna that recommends a good long-term cheap hotel. And find a place to sleep immediately. Good plan on throat sore and no sleep and thirty-five thousand of this strange money patting down my inside breast pocket. My suitcase won't really fit inside the telephone box. Or it's just that the two of us can't fit in there together so my phone concentration isn't all it should be and then of course I don't speak German, and English is, well, not the preferred language.

I sorted it out. I mean when you win big the first night, everything gets itself sorted out. I got my own apartment. It wasn't really close to the card room, but I had a pass for unlimited use of public transport and in Vienna they have buses, subways, and streetcars.

Apartment's a bit strong. I mean, there was a kitchen and a living room and an entranceway and a bathroom, but there was nothing in any of them. No furniture, no stuff, and no lights. Just a light in the entranceway and one in the bathroom. And a chair and a table and a couch that was made into a bed with sheets on it and a folded blanket at the foot of it in the living room. But it was cheap, I had my own key, and I could come and go as I pleased. Anyway, I won the first night. Bed, sleep, good night.

I ended up staying in Vienna about a month that trip. In the end at least I got my confidence back. And a sense of order. After that first night, we didn't play 500-1000 limit much, the main game was the 250-500 schilling Hold'em. But that was a rocking little game, and at the end of a month I felt like everything made sense again. Again.

POKER'S GOOD IF you like watching people. Not if you like people because then you won't like people so much. But people-watching, watching people who are drunk or scared or angry or with really big ears and fish face or just plain sitting there and thinking, What's up with that guy? What's his deal? Nooo way. And most people are too wrapped up in their own troubles to care—just how much am I up or how much I'm down.

I'm a watcher. Always have been. Maybe that's why I learned. I love to watch people, love to stare at 'em behind my dark shades as they load up racks with new-found dollars and walk away. Or as they fall apart, as they crumble up, as their eyes become big and glassy and lose focus and they take deep drags on their cigarettes. As they come in all smiles and how ya doing and start winning and talk about how good they are and how they could have made an extra bet by checking the flop, and then a month later they're stuck on the rail trying to borrow money from the same guys they called losers a little while before. I just watch. Don't say nothing. Nothing. Just sit there and watch 'em night after night with a big silly grin on my face as they call me a live one.

Player asks, How's my game, man, my game? Your game? Who gives a fuck about your game, I want to know what you're gonna do when they're fuckin' breathing down your neck they got you hooked so good and you're so scared you're praying you ain't got a pair when you look down at those hole cards because Krock he just raised again with a queen up, and even though you know he's got shit, you know it, man, I could fuckin' swear it down to my bones. If I look down and see a pair of sickly eights my stomach is just turning, 'cause I don't want to get there in no pot with him, man, where the river card is a big black snake and fate has already decided which cards are in that deck and which order they come out and odds in my favor has much less meaning to me than the pain in my stomach that feels like the lining is getting eaten away by acid—at least that feels real. I don't know how the odds feel.

You really need a lot of money to play poker. A lot lot. So much that if you had it all you might as well not play anymore, unless you got nothing else to do or are just out for blood money.

Two WEEKS BEFORE I left for Asia I hit a little run. I hadn't even thought I was gonna play any more cards, just pack up Jimmy's and my house near Atlantic City and go. But wouldn't you know I went in. And I hit 'em so good that one time I raised on a straight and flush draw on the turn even though the odds were against me because I just knew it was coming and it did and when I'm raking the pot Johnny World makes a wry comment about me raising on the turn and I just want to say, World, if you'd just come through everything the same way I did, then you'd be raising in that spot too. Anyway, it was nice to have a small cushion for the trip.

Ah. Being away from poker . . . That's what was nice. Eight solid months of sitting on beaches and buses and nothing to do but think. Think about poker and reorient myself, and put some order in. Playing events round and round in my head and seeing leering faces in my mind, and then sitting with those leering faces and seeing what the angles were. What I could have said, what I should have done, when I should have quit, and how I could have played. I'm a great reviewer. I'm a world champion after the fact. But if you don't sit with it you aren't gonna learn from it, and perspective is the master teacher.

I thought a lot about Bart and a lot about John Smiley. And all of the sudden it seemed to me that, in poker, people don't get what's coming to them. They only get what they take.

And I thought how plain I could now see that great play doesn't always make great dollars. Some nights I would jump out of bed tense as a board, walk out to my porch, and spend hours. Just sitting there.

It's funny how perspective goes. It's funny how sitting there in my chair staring out over the blue water and the funky clouds I could see the poker table more clearly than when I was there. I could see Bart's eyes, I could see John Smiley's white clenched fist, I could still see the cards and the hands and everybody's movements and listen to their words over and over, and it changed me. Lying there on my favorite rock letting the sun wash over me I learned more about those poker games in Atlantic City than I ever learned sitting at that cramped table under the flood of artificial lights.

I went a lot of places, but the best part of my trip was the three months that I spent in Nepal. That's where I learned to do a little yoga. Yoga's not really weird. It's kind of like doing toe touches in the morning. Except in yoga you try and touch your toes and then stay there for a while. At least that's how I do it. It sure feels good stretching out when you spend the rest of your time sitting in a chair with a knot in your stomach.

LIVE
ONE

IT'S NEVER REAL. I mean there is no reality away from the poker table, because there you try to paraphrase it to make parables because everyone says, What is it? How is it? What it is. Isn't it crazy? It's the easy life and it's nothing that can be explained, because the explanation changes with the day and the game and how you're doing and all I can think is that after six years of getting it together and eight solid months of sun and reflection to get it together and get focused and get healthy and breathe deeply then I come to Amsterdam and get in a big game and feel great and calm and powerful and I get cold fuckin' decked out of fifteen thousand dollars. Just like that. Not a chance. Don't let the door hit you in the ass, said the three can't-fuckin'-play Germans who took my money for four days straight. No, they didn't say that. They said, Are you through, as I went all in for yet another time and then got up from the table and stuffed the few chips that I had left, which were considered too worthless to even put in the pot. And then they laughed in my face. And then I went back to my hotel and went to sleep. That's the reality of poker.

I been playing for over six years now—AC, Vegas, California, Connecticut, Europe—and I still try and start each day as a new day, pick myself off the floor and get focused. Like one night with the Pinster, who's a poker champion, probably the best in Europe and I mean this guy is really smart, he can see right through your cards. We're sitting next to each other in a Pot-Limit Hold'em game and he wins a big pot, doubles his stack, and I say to him, "Well, that's a nice little lead to stake yourself to this early in the night."

He says, "What do you mean, lead? I'm still stuck two thousand marks."

"Whadaya mean?" I say. "I saw you buy in for only five hundred . . ."

"No, I'm still counting from yesterday."

I give a laugh. "So, is that how it goes. Well, then, I guess I'm stuck about fifty thousand or so. . . ." But you gotta see what I mean. You can't worry about what happened. The important things are to be in action, to have a bankroll, to be focused, and to be in a good game, maybe in that order. And maybe that's why I'm still here after losing eighteen times in a row last year, and after calling that guy for a thousand marks last night when he had a flush and I had a pair of aces. And I mean the guy never laid one bluff down all night, especially not for that size, and you'd have to really be an idiot to make that call. But I did it and I lost my money and I was pretty hot at myself, but you know this morning I feel okay. I forgive myself and I'm ready to go back in and play the hell out of those cards and I ain't trying to get even, I'm just trying to make some money. Starting right now. That's how you gotta think about it. Gotta do it that way or it eats you up inside and you blow off about ten thousand marks just being mad at yourself for the first thousand. I seen it happen too many times.

EVERYTHING CONVERGED ON Atlantic City that week. Me. Four boxes of crazy clothes. A hoard of people with money to burn. And the blizzard of '96. . . .

Presidents' Day is an interesting holiday. Because it's one of those holidays that no one celebrates but everyone has off work and there's no family obligations and it's right after the big holidays and the new year and everybody's got money and bonuses and nothing to do. Consequently, it's like the biggest gambling weekend of the year.

I haven't been in Atlantic City for over nine months, long time for a guy who was there day after day, almost every day for a year, and I knew it was gonna be weird. I'd done so much thinking, so much thinking, so much time on the beach with a bong staring up at the stars. At the millions of stars, sitting out on my porch on an island in Thailand at 10 P.M., when the stars were so bright because there were no other lights, and it's like being in a real big room because it's all your room, and then you're just in the room with your mind. And they, of course, meanwhile they'd been spending all their time in Atlantic City in the Taj Mahal poker room over in the corner in the high-limit section with the same exact faces days and on the weekends and for the holidays and at 3 A.M. And some go broke and some get lucky and the only for sure is that the house is gonna take their cut and believe me it's gonna hurt you.

All the crazy clothes I ever wore plus the crazier ones I bought in Asia. My box of crazy hats plus my whiller wham 'em three-foot-tall royal purple velvet Dr. Seuss hat, which I'm saving to wear with my new royal purple cashmere double-breasted suit with the custom-made twelve-inch bell-bottom cuffs, and when I put those on with my Himalayan mountain climber mirror wraparound sunglasses and stroll into the poker room freshly showered and surprise them in a game at four in the morning, stuck, tired, and whatever, I'm gonna fuck 'em up.

I got into town surrounding some pretty rugged conditions. Cold and windy. And no reservation. I figured I had a couple things going for me. My contacts, good relations with the Taj Mahal poker staff, and the fact that there's always an extra room. I just had to get it. Besides, I got a wallet full of money, and the action, the action has to be good. I'll figure it out.

Man, they started talking up that blizzard days in advance. All that we knew was that if it happened it'd be sometime around the weekend. How magnificently convenient, I was gonna get there first.

I drove into the Taj Mahal parking lot with a bundle of money, four suitcases, and a box of hats. Wednesday afternoon. Felt just like old times. Took me twelve minutes to get into action. I left all my stuff in the car while checking out the poker room and found a 100-200 Stud game that couldn't be beat. They'd been playing all night. I hadn't seen anybody in a year, Fresca Kid and Tofu Trina and Louie and two characters I'd never seen before. I went right up to the table, expecting to be hailed like the conquering hero. I mean after all, I'd spent a lot of time with these people.

"Hi, Trina." Blank look.

"Oh, hi, Mickey, where you been . . ." I launch a few wisecracks and start a story. No response. Then, "Look, I'm sorry, but I been playing all night and I'm kind of tired, all right?"

That's when I got the picture. They really had been playing all night. Stop fooling around and get in the fuckin' game. I shut up and sat down. Deal 'em up, shooter. But the game is in its dying throes. Both of the unknowns quit within an hour and I decide to take care of practical matters.

They could only give me a room for the night. It was gonna be packed solid this weekend. But I got good friends with Paulette at the reservations desk and some of the floor people must've put in a good word or something. She said I was on the top of the list if something opened up, check back tomorrow around eleven. And then there was the blizzard.

Now to check in. I know what I want. I want to be high up, high, because at the Taj they have this tower that goes all the way up fifty-two floors, and the views up at the top are tremendous. Right off into the ocean. Or down the boardwalk. Or out into the Atlantic City wastelands.

Bingo. A friendly girl at the desk sets me up on the fiftieth floor. Big bed. Pink rug. Hot shower. I've gotta start it out kind of slow, I mull over the shower and some yoga. Gotta get some pot.

It turns out Jimmy's in town, upstairs sleeping off a long poker session. We haven't seen each other in quite a while and a little bit of catching up is in order. He gets himself together and we head out for a Vietnamese feast. People are creepy, Jimmy says. Man, just about everybody you got to watch out for now. Partnerships, teams, pieces, going short in pots, the money just ain't the same that it used to be. Jimmy and I always talk about getting out of the business. Poker's taking too much out of our stomachs, and it's hard to stay good in a world of steadily crumbling values. We just want to play if the money's there. Or that's what we say.

It's hard for most people to talk about poker. I mean it's easy to say, Oh yeah, man, and listen to bad beat stories and how some guy had two queens and got beat on the last card by a guy that raised him drawing almost dead and say, Tsk, man, you're really running bad. Because that's all that most guys want to talk about. But Jimmy and I see eye to eye about poker. We don't ever talk about bad beat stories and griping. Because it's all just shit. We look at the game the same way, the business, and we're always talking about the big picture, talking about ethics, talking about angles. We take the luck part of the game and stick it in a big cage laced with a lot of humor. Who wants to put sense into something completely senseless.

Jimmy's leaving town in the morning. He's been at the Taj Mahal for two weeks straight and needs a little time off. His eyes have that glazed-over look that you get from too much action and too little sleep.

Jimmy and I saunter into the card room full from a Vietnamese dinner. Man, Jimmy knows where to eat and what to get. There's a 100-200 Hold'em going on but it's shit, we both find that out as soon as we sit down. Poodles has the money and he's playing tight and Captain Tom's got his iron fist clamped on the game, and the live ones are looking bored and Porky's there looking all stuck and live and not wanting to play Hold'em—he can't shoot as many angles there.

We start talking about starting up another game, a game that'll have some action, that'll get people gambling, and we decide we should start a three- or four-way, that is three or four different games. Everybody's dicking around about committing and so it finally ends up being just me and Jimmy and Porky over at a new table trying to attract the action from the next way over. There's an Asian kid named Jung who's been in from California for a few days. He's a Hold'em player, but we don't think he can play the other games for shit. He knows too much in that Hold'em ring game and he's looking bored to boot.

I'm not too thrilled about playing with just these two guys. Especially not since we are having to play 150-300 limit to not "interfere" with the 100-200 Hold'em game at the next table. 150-300 is really high but I've agreed to do it for an hour or two just to see if we can get this game going. We play about two or three hands when a buddy swings by to see if I want to "take a break." I do.

"Look, guys," I say, "I gotta go somewhere for about fifteen minutes, then I'll be right back. But I'm leaving my chips here and I am gonna play." They aren't so happy about it but Jimmy is like, okay, Mickey, he knows I'm being straight with him.

It doesn't take long to get connected. There's a whole bevy

of poker players who like to smoke pot and everyone's cool and I'm sharing a joint in someone's room and later I've got my own bag, complete with a free pair of kooky sunglasses because my man knows I like weird stuff. These sunglasses have a big pair of fluorescent rolly eyes painted on the lenses that make me look ghoulish.

Anyway it's only been fifteen minutes and I'm not really thinking too much about what is gonna happen between Jimmy and Porky during those fifteen minutes, and if I did think about it I'd laugh thinking how Jimmy's gonna torture that boy.

I slip back down into my seat with an "All right, here I am," and Jimmy, man, Jimmy barely pays me notice, and he is hot. He just antes for the next hand. Porky, fuckin' dog ass Porky is up in his chair and he's so goofy happy he's just trying to keep the laughter in, but it's coming out in short bursts. Man, he thinks everything is funny. He looks up at me and laughs.

They're playing Seven Stud Hilo. I ante up and play about two hands and a new dealer comes into the box. Time to play Hold'em. Porky picks a rack up off the floor and starts to stack his chips. I give Jimmy the cross-eyed and furrowed brow.

"What the fuck do you think you're doing?" Jimmy asks him.

"I don't really want to play anymore," Porky says and he giggles.

"What?" I say. "What the hell happened while I was gone?" Porky got lucky, no doubt about that one. "What's up, Jimmy?"

"What's up? I'll tell you what's up, this lying motherfucker is one slimy ass bastard, I'll tell you, man. First he gets me to

take a third of him just to get the game started, and now that
he's beat me out of thirty-five hundred in ten minutes he
wants to hit and run."

"Hold it. . . . What? You got a piece of this guy? Jimmy,
what are you thinking about, brother?" I mean Jimmy is my
best friend on earth, but this is so stupid it's funny. I'm sorry,
but I'm laughing up all over the place. "Man, I ain't been
here in nine months and look what's happening." People getting low on down.

"Yeah, but I'm just trying to get the game started. Who
knows the motherfucker is looking to hit-and-run me. . . ."

"Yeah, I know what you're saying. . . ."

What a slime ball this Porky is. He asks Jimmy to take a
third of him because he don't want to play so high and Jimmy
says okay just to get the game started but then when they
start playing head up it's completely ridiculous because
Jimmy is always being forced to bet half of his money dead
against himself. So now Porky gets lucky to boot and cleans
him out of five thousand in fifteen minutes. And then wants
to quit Jimmy. To give him no shot at his money. Fifteen
minutes after he asks Jimmy to give him money to put in
action. That Jimmy gave him for the sole reason that Porky
would play for long enough to see if the game gets started. I
mean it ain't that Jimmy likes Porky's game. There's nothing
in any rule book about this situation. But you have to make
your own lines. Why do you think I'm done with taking
pieces?

Porky's just sitting there with that stupid smile, like his
hand's just been caught in the cookie jar, but he don't care
because he just ate the cookie. What a goof. His long fingers
shuffle his chips in that jerky fashion, he's always jerking

around with his little bag of oranges and bananas that he swiped from the buffet because they were free, shooting the angles.

"Man, Jimmy, this poker room's full of some dirty fuckin' people." That makes him smile.

He looks at me and can't help but laugh. "This motherfucker is so sneaky, man, he's creepy." And he shivers a little bit.

Now Porky's trying to press some sort of advantage. "Well, let's make it all Hilo then, just two games."

"You're full of shit, Porky, you agreed to play three games to try and start it, this is fuckin' ridiculous."

Porky says, "Well . . ." and giggles. Man, he repulses me.

We just sit there arguing for a while. Jimmy's hot and I think Porky's a slime ball, but nothing is getting accomplished and we're all just sitting there. We got no place to go. Except Porky is thinking about his video poker addiction, and now that he's ahead a few thousand for the day how nice and relaxing it would be to sit there and play ninety hands a minute of five quarter video poker and sit there hunched forward in a chair over the video poker machine, eyes glued to the flashing screen and fingers punching buttons at a hundred miles an hour.

Just when Porky's about got his mind made up to go and Jimmy and I are about done abusing the stupid old dog ass, DB waltzes up out of thin air and slides into the seat next to Porky and puts a huge roll of bills down on the table and says, "What's this game, boys?" It's three-way. DB says, "Add Stud and I'll play four-way," and now that we got another player Porky has kind of got no choice, and he don't want to play, but if he don't Jimmy's looking like there might be a fight.

Well, I don't like this spot so much, but now we're rolling, and we're just trying to lure the Asian kid and some others over, anyway. He's got like less than no chance playing Omaha. . . .

It's a few hours later. The Hold'em game is broken and dead, scattered to the wind the moment Jung decided to stop pouring money into it. In one long thin motion he jumped up from his chair, picked up his stack of cash, stuffed his few chips in his pocket, moved one table over to take a seat in our 150-300 game, and sent the room and the night, for that matter, spinning. Now everybody had to play four games. The winners quit and the losers changed games and for a while we had ourselves an eight handed four-way 150-300 game. When I've lost two buy-ins and most of my third, I know it's time to go to my room. Right now the game can only stew.

Do yoga. Stand on my head. Take a shower and smoke a joint. Get dressed. Faded blue and red striped knit cap that I picked up for three bucks in a Bangkok market and liked it so much that I went back a month later for two more. Turn the air up high and get my money and my plan and the door closes behind me with a click.

What's gonna be going on in the game when I get back down there? Well, I hope DB has quit, for one thing. He was ahead and he's playing good and I don't want him tonight. I want the guys who are stuck.

I walk into the poker room and all eyes are upon me but I slip into my seat with no acknowledgments and count the piddly skittling of chips in front of my place. What the hell do I care, I want the money that's on the table. First thing I notice is the Asian guy is on tilt. Man, is he ever looking like a jumping bean. Porky has just won a bunch of pots and I know this because he's sitting back in his chair picking his finger-nails with his pocketknife. He's got a calm goofy smile on his face and he sits there for about thirty seconds trying to think up something sarcastic and witty to say and then comes out with, "So where's that hat from?"

I look down for about two seconds and move my chips a little and then grab two chips and lift my arm up in the air and slam my fist down on the table, clacking my chips. Then I look up and stare right at him with my mirror sunglasses and don't say anything. Then I kick my legs around a little and look down and don't say anything. I either want him mad at me or out of the game. He gives a shrug-me-off chuckle and goes back to his nails. He's too happy about being ahead to rock right now.

Jimmy's at the other end of the table with his cool rider mask on. But his body is tensed up over the table and he must be fuming because of the shit with Porky and running so bad tonight and two weeks of shit and I think he just wants to get even and go upstairs. For that matter so do I. But I'm gonna stay and play as long as I think the game's good. And it's very good right now. But then, Jimmy and I always could start up a good game.

I GUESS IT was fitting that I came into town surrounding some pretty rugged conditions. I mean my thoughts on poker were pretty rugged, especially considering the universal disre-

gard for my game that I had found everywhere except in a
few select enclaves and of course my own mind, where I was
riding high on my thoughts about poker and the scene and
my ability to convert it into cash. Or this is how I thought
about it at my good times.

In my bad times I think, How bad do I really play? Or, Do I
really play bad? Or am I a victim of some weird fate? But
everyone's gotta find out how the story ends. I mean you've
got to keep going as long as you get just enough encouragement. Even if you get a lot of disappointments, warnings,
disasters. If you get just enough encouragement along the way
at the right times, and I'm talking about staying in money,
then you just keep going. Because if you never won then you'd
never really play that much. You just wouldn't last that long.
Everyone's reality is a victim of their own experience. So
another night goes and I sit there and watch my money go
drip drip away. Nice hand. That's good. You win. Nothing else
to say. I can't help thinking I can play poker. That's where
this money comes from.

All right, so I don't really play like I used to play. I don't
even play close to the way I used to play. And I guess I'm the
only one who thinks I play better. I think I play a lot better.
Only I'm doing a lot worse. It's not like I don't make a lot of
mistakes. I do. But mistakes are subjective. You have to forgive yourself for them, I think, or else you get hung up on
them. You just can't always be making the same mistakes
again.

The next day I'm thrown back in the shit again. I quit the
game when the Fresca Kid showed up all fresh and it was just
him and Jimmy and me and Jung and I was loser four thousand. Jimmy said he was gonna keep playing and then drive

straight home. My room got extended for one more night, and thank God because I don't get to sleep until after noon and then try as I might I can't sleep for any more than five hours. Bounce awake out of a poker dream and try to make sense of the red numbers shining off the alarm clock. I'm still tired. Of course that doesn't mean I'm going back to sleep. Not before checking out the poker room. Not seeing as how I'm already stuck for the trip and action's going on downstairs. Shower and prowl . . .

WE'VE BEEN PLAYING 100-200 Hold'em for most of the night, but about one-thirty we switch to two games, half Hold'em and half Omaha Hilo, to keep Floyd and Porky from quitting, to prevent the game from breaking when it's getting short-handed.

Goren comes over like a whirlwind, putting a large roll of bills down in the ten seat exactly in time to receive the big blind. Mirrored sunglasses. Sporty dress. He's new in town, wasn't here a year ago, a Hold'em specialist, but I think he's been on a good run since he got here. Young guy, I got him figured for like a 15-30 California Hold'em player who's been here a few weeks hit-and-running the soft 30-60 and 50-100 and higher Hold'em and pumping his roll and he's super focused and aggressive for short plays, always putting hundreds in the pot, never changing in for chips the guy doesn't even take his jacket off when he plays, one eye is always on the door and he's always thinking about the money. Eyes on the money. That's good and bad. I played Hold'em with him last night but he didn't play for long just got real lucky and picked up a few thousand in ten minutes and bye-bye, boys. He's got me figured for a major live one. Of that I'm positive, if he even thinks about that stuff.

Goren gets outkickered one hand and then ole Porky makes a flush on his ass and he's stuck—good one—maybe tonight he's gonna stick around a little. Let's see if he plays Omaha. The new dealer comes in and Goren says, "What is this shit? Let's make it all Hold'em."

"I object!" Snarly voice. I'm stuffing this one in the bucket. "We're playing two games." I'm looking right at him, sunglasses to sunglasses. Come get me, pretty boy. He makes a disgusted look on his face and the dealer looks up at me. "All right, Paul, you're dealing Omaha Hilo." All right. I know he can't leave. And he don't want to play Omaha.

And he don't know how to play Omaha. I mean he might pass on guts and instinct in a ring game, but we're short-handed and things can get weird here if you don't know the big picture.

Now I'm getting interested. I had started off running bad in the game, real bad, and now I go all in for the third time tonight, three thousand dollars up in smoke. I take out the crumpled bills that are in my right front pocket. Exactly a thousand dollars. How convenient. I toss it in front of me with a sharp exhale of breath, like I'm fighting for control. I'm a little hot, but I like this game, like my edge, and like my focus.

Louie is sitting right on my left, raking my chips with them last-card draw-outs. Hey, boy, last card ain't gonna get you there every time. Floyd has been looking to go since he won the first hand when he sat down six hours ago, and he quits winner for the night. I drift down and out, gotta wait for my time. . . .

The game drones on, the only good news being that Goren is entrenched, he ain't getting even and now we made it through two rounds of Hold'em and this is our second time playing Omaha and it's the longest I ever seen him play. He pushed that last ace-jack he got in Hold'em way too hard, so I'm thinking he's desperate. I'm ready to let him bluff at me, and I'm just stalking him down. Can't get a hand, can't get a hand, pay off a bad one and I only got about six hundred in front of me when we change to Hold'em and Porky and Louie quit winners. Now we're three-handed and I hit a few hands in a row and just destroy them in three-player Hold'em. Blue Ned only had about sixteen hundred in front of him when the round started and when he goes all in he just pushes his chair back and says, "See ya." Goren doesn't say anything, just puts his blind in for the next hand. He's mad, hot as a firecracker, and he's got his roll of bills clenched in his hand, he just counted them again. Yeah, I'll play head up.

We only got about seven minutes left of Hold'em and I'm gonna clamp it up, make sure he don't get any money or confidence back before the Omaha Hilo round. Sure enough, we just trade blinds back and forth for a few minutes, nobody says nothing and then the dealer gets a tap and there's a new dealer and he says, "C'mon, let's play Hold'em, you can't play Omaha head up. . . ."

I know I'm being an asshole, I want him to feel asshole from me. I look down and say, "No! I want to play two games. We'll play Hold'em again in half an hour!"

He's got that disgusted look on his face again, like I'm being the baby. You bet I am. I know he don't want to play Omaha. And I know he can't quit me.

Fuck, what the hell do I know about Omaha Hilo either, except that you gotta play tight, can't be playing every hand just because it's split pot. That's not a very advanced strategy. But I got the cards and it worked.

Worked because poor Goren had no idea what was going on, and there I am sitting with the stone-cold nuts about five hands in a row, and he figures he's gotta bluff me because he ain't got anything and, man, it got pretty messy with him slamming his fist on the table and throwing the cards and twice when I called him at the end he didn't even want to show his hand he just called out, "Nothing."

We get to Hold'em and I win the first pot and he's only got about two hundred and fifty bucks left in front of him, I've beaten him for about three thousand this half hour and wouldn't you know I'm not even stuck for the night anymore, I'm up two thousand. How things change.

I look at the dealer. "Hold it up." Now I sideways look over at Goren. "I'm willing to keep playing for a while, but you gotta take out more money." And I look down at my chips and wait. Like I'm gonna let him take a shot at the six thousand I got sitting on the table for only two hundred and fifty dollars. How do I know how much he's got in his pocket? I learned this lesson from a master.

"Who the fuck are you kidding?"

"I don't mind either way. I'm just saying if you want me to keep playing you're gonna have to take some more money out."

"Well, I gotta go to my box."

"That's all right. I don't mind waiting."

"I don't fuckin' believe this. I'm gonna remember this." A quick look. Then he grabs up his scattering and heads for the door without looking back. I just feel, mean.

FRIDAY MORNING THE blizzard hit. Snow started coming down but some people were still coming in, like dealers and floor people and a few players. Nobody really knew that they wouldn't be going home. Door to the gas chamber lies open, ladies and gentlemen. Nothing but greasy buffets and the Portobello mushroom burger from room service along with maybe the Tuscan salad, and pot. A whole lot of pot, and I made sure I tipped the maid good and said, Do you think it's possible I might have a few extra towels? So now I got like a gym's inventory of towels in the bathroom and I'm taking at least six or seven or ten hot showers a day and padding back and forth down the silent mirrored corridors to the elevator and the poker room and back up to my room. And I pace around a little bit and do a lot of talking to myself and do yoga and put on my dark glasses and go back down to the poker room. And so does everyone else. And every time, I smoke a joint and change my clothes and change my hat. And make a plan. And tell myself I'm the man.

It snows all the time, but this is a special one. We started hearing stories about five o'clock. The last of the dealers are coming in, the ones on swing shift who don't live too far

away. It's bad out there, they say, cars are doing donuts. I'm
wearing an old wool blazer that I picked up at the Salvation
Army, but I put it in the washing machine and then the dryer
to clean it and I kind of had an accident. Now it looks a little
like a rag. My mom keeps trying to throw it out every time
I'm home. But it still fits me, and it's got pockets.

I can't sleep and I can't stay awake. I look down at my
cards. Jack-six. Another fold. I'm bored and I want to gamble.
Ah, don't think about none of that. Here come the cards.

I've spent the day in a stoned stupor and a tight-ass ten-
handed 50-100 Hold'em game. I haven't been to sleep yet,
staring at the ceiling for a while in the morning until I came
down and found a bunch who had just come into town. I'm
fluctuating between stuck about two and three thousand. For
the trip that is. Jung's sitting over in the big Stud game where
he's been since sometime yesterday. His nose is opened, but
otherwise it's a tough-looking Stud game, 150-300. Captain
Tom's talking to me and Jung and DB about starting up a
higher game, only Hold'em, but I ain't making no commit-
ments to him. Captain Tom don't give nothing up in Hold'em
and I don't want to play short with him and DB in the same
game because I think they might be going partners. Jimmy
told me to keep my eyes open for everything. I've now been
up so long and smoked so much pot that even that is hard
lately.

I ain't sleeping. I mean sometimes I doze between hands,
sometimes a lot. The game's slow, a ring game, and you don't
have to watch as much so often when you know the players.
You should, but when you're playing twelve hours and nineteen out of every twenty-four, then you gotta zone out a little
so you can have a zone to zone back into. I like the surreal

dance, always have, of being able to sink back into time and nothingness, put my head on my elbow like I'm sleeping, crack my eyes open a bare bit, and try to make all my other senses completely aware. And just feel the game, feel its pulse, what's happening, and where emotions are at. And get some winks.

At least one guy is as tired as me. I don't think fuckin' Jung has been to sleep yet since I met him. Or maybe once. Anyway, he's still wearing that tan suit. Guy must be starting to wish he had some more clothes. Can't tell if he's seventeen or thirty-seven, but I guess he's right about between. This fellow has got a ton of gamble in him. He really had his nose opened up playing the four-way game the other night. Fat lot of good it did me. I had to try hard to lose four thousand. I definitely want to play those games with him again.

Of course you'd never find Captain Tom in a combination game. Jimmy and I call him a nit. Oh, there's a lot of nits around. Look, there's a lot worse things than being a nit. I mean the Captain's a winner, for one thing. But he's a Hold'em specialist, and I think he's got it all figured out in that Larry Sandtrap type of way of bets per hour and win rate. He does a lot of things right, like he knows to stick around when the game's good and he tries to be real popular, no, what am I saying, he is real popular 'cause he has an easy smile and a laugh and he's got a special nickname for all the regulars and people that just come down to play on the weekends. Everyone wants to be in Captain Tom's game and he always says, Looking sharp tonight, Mick, when he sees me in my big ole brown suit that I found in the attic of the house Jimmy and I rented. But really he's the one who's looking sharp, or always trying to, in his brand-new sport coat with tailored pants and his manicured hands and not a hair out of place and his hundred-dollar sunglasses. But he does have an effect on people—they want to be like him, they want to play like him, and they wanna sit next to him to be his confidant, his respected peer. And so when some dude in the one seat plays the queen-deuce off suit and wins a pot and Tom shakes his head sadly and snorts scornfully and with raised eyebrows says in a low voice, Did you see that? maybe he'll be speaking to you and therefore implying that since he's talking to you, you know better and Captain Tom thinks you're a good player and you're not a live one like the dude in the corner.

There's not a human being alive who plays Hold'em as tight as Captain Tom. He can sit there for hours, I mean hours, and just fold every hand, and he seems to think that's all there is to it. Who am I to say, maybe that is all there is, but I just wish he wouldn't try and draw so much attention to the damn thing. I mean the guy's actually proud about the fact that everybody knows him as the tightest player in the room. He likes that when he walks in everyone says, There's Captain Tom, the tightest Hold'em player on the planet, and if someone raises and Captain Tom reraises then half the table stands up and some guy says with mock incredulity, Did Captain Tom reraise? And the guy who's still in the hand quakes in his boots and mucks his hand fast, and Captain Tom smiles and takes the pot and maybe shows it or not, but the man has the goods.

He's proud of that respect he's earned. So he raises and everyone folds. But me I'm thinking to myself, What the fuck good is that? I mean the whole point is to get people to call when you got a good hand, not fold. And who wants to give action to someone who gives no action? Who in their right

mind would gamble with someone who ain't gambling themselves? Which is why I don't play with Tom so much anymore
and why we invented the three-way game and why for a
while during the evolution of the Taj Mahal poker room you
would walk into the high-limit section and there might be a
limit Hold'em game, and then there would be a combination
game.

But the main difference is never just the particular form of
poker being played. No. Because maybe they'll be playing
50-100 Hold'em or maybe it's 75-150 but Captain Tom will be
in the ten seat and a couple of his cronies or fellow nits will be
spread around the table and it might even be a full game, or
in fact it probably is because a lot of people enjoy playing
with Tom. But when you get up close to the table and stand
there for five minutes all I can tell you is this—it ain't no
poker game, it's a fucking coffee klatsch, and they ain't no
gamblers but just a bunch of old biddies clickety-clack gossip-
ing over a handful of small change. And why? Well, they're
all sitting around there and everyone's trying to play like
Captain Tom, by which I mean everybody's got the ole tire
iron clamped down on their play and folding every hand so
there may be ten guys in the game but the average pot has
just two or three guys in it. Just the raiser and the blinds who
have to be in anyway, and half the time there's not even a
flop or the pot goes check and fold on the first card, so the pots
are all piddly small. And if for some reason a pot gets big,
maybe six guys in the hand and a couple raises, you can be
sure it's because someone got dealt aces and someone's got
kings or there's set over set or just some kind of crazy fluke
that happens because hand after hand is being dealt and the
laws of probability bend and sway.

And God help the poor soul who gets out of line in that game and manages to crack someone's two kings with a moron two pair or back-door flush, because he ain't never gonna hear the end of it. I mean the guy might get the pot, but he's made to feel like they're getting out the branding iron from the hot coals and emblazoning a bright S for sucker on his forehead. And when he looks up and around the table he feels like Hester Prynne and the money feels empty because all around the table he gets dark looks and pointing fingers and whispering and now no one will talk to him and he can't take part in the table discussion about standard deviations or a particular rule clarification or whether Captain Tom would have reraised in that spot with the two tens or if he put him on ace-queen.

So that's the kind of game I been playing in for the last seven hours, and I'm beginning to wonder why I just don't go up and go to sleep. I mean it is Friday afternoon, I've been up since about six o'clock yesterday and this game has no action and everybody's fresh and I can really sleep on them. It's a good time to really sleep on them. I look around the table, alert faces, eager about the weekend, happy to be out of the snow. I'm almost a dog in this game, I think as I look down a little bit too hard at a six-eight of clubs before sticking it in the muck. And they got this time pot thing.

Once the game gets past a certain limit the house doesn't take money out of the pot. Instead the casino charges every player in the game per half hour—to pay for the dealer and the service. This is how the house makes their money. In the 50-100 game at the Taj, for example, the time charge is nine dollars per player for every half hour—paid every time a new dealer comes into the box. In some games players agree that the first person to win a big pot, say over five hundred dollars, pays time for the whole table, or ninety dollars. It's not a bad idea when you're playing 50-100 and all you got on the table is green twenty-five-dollar chips and so for the dealer to have to go around the whole table and make exact change for everyone—and some dealers are slow—it might take them five minutes and all you want from them is to shut up and deal and get out as many hands as possible and in the grand scheme everyone's gonna pay time so let's just get it over with and get on with the game.

Yeah, right. Because in Captain Tom's tight-ass game you've never seen so many guys trying to weasel out of nine dollars per half hour so often and so many of those nits play such long hours and so many times per week and for them poker is just like punching the time clock and dollars per hour so it becomes a competition not to have to pay the time and the effect on the game is that it becomes even tighter—yeah, can you believe it—and everyone is so scared to win a big pot and have to pay ninety dollars that they won't play any hand at all and a guy will say, Oh, is this a time pot? And then fold. Everyone's counting every pot and sometimes it'll take fifteen minutes before a pot gets over five hundred dollars because every time it gets to four hundred the betting stops and it's check check check and I sure haven't seen Captain Tom pay too many of them. I mean he must just fold every hand and figure as long as he never pays time then he's always playing for free. And yes, that makes sense, but how can you expect to make any money in a game where everything you say and do is designed to make people clam up and gambling the big S word for seven deadly sins? In the early days it was possible because there was so much money around you couldn't even chase it away with a stick, but as time went on, Captain Tom and guys like him seemed to be playing in the bad games, in the tight games. The only way you can make money in that spot is to be lucky or else to shoot angles.

So why don't I go now? Why don't I just get up from the table and take my cash and stuff? Because you can't get even when you're sleeping. Jung's called it quits over in the Stud game. He left the room so fast I never saw him get up. Louie's in the room, on the list. Porky ain't showed up yet. Or Floyd.

Times like this is when I get depressed at the poker table. Depressed because there's no money and everybody is click clackety around and I'm losing and I start to look at everybody at the table and the house taking the money and the old-timers playing a little lower than they used to and not winning quite so much. And the new guys, the ones that ain't been in poker so long, are the ones running good and getting the money and on the hot streaks. And everyone's going broke. Well, almost everyone. It just depends when the eventual ends.

Word's come in that the roads are being closed. Stuck in Atlantic City. It doesn't look like many more people are going to be showing up for the weekend. Not anymore. Snow kept them away. I'm losing about a thousand in the game, stuck thirty-five hundred or so for the trip so far. And the weekend's just beginning. I take off my sunglasses and rub my face with both hands. Push my chair back and stand up slowly, start to put my chips in the pocket of my blazer. Captain Tom perks up.

"Ya quittin', Mick? What's wrong, Mick, you don't like the game?"

"I'm tired, Tom. I'm really tired. I been up since yesterday.

I'm just gonna get a few hours' sleep and I'll, uh, see you guys in a while."

"Yeah, all right, you do that, eh, Mick. Me and the boys here will, eh, keep the game going for you. Maybe later we'll, eh, pump up the limit a couple notches. That'd be nice, huh? You'd like that, eh, Mick?"

"Yeah, we'll see, Tom. Right now I'm just gonna go to sleep."

"All right. Nice playing with you, eh, Mick. See you later."

"Thanks, Tom, uh, good luck to you. Good luck." To the rest of the table and I take my chips and I'm staggering away, Captain Tom nice enough to wait until I get out of earshot before the snide remarks begin. At least that's how it is with everyone else. Can't guess I'm much different. Seat open.

JUMP AWAKE heart pounding. Ugh . . . 2:35. I sit up in bed and lean back against the wall, trying to get it all together. 2:38. I turn on the lamp next to me. Close and open my eyes a few times. Hotel room. What was I dreaming about? Weird poker stuff. There's an infomercial on the TV. Some kind of exerciser. Gotta get up. . . . Gotta go check out the games. I kind of drift off, awake, dozing. 2:53. No, now I'm up. I shake my head and get out of bed and head right into the shower where I cough for about three minutes. Gotta stop smoking cigarettes. Shower is pleasure. Wonder what ac-

tion is happening in the poker room. It can't still be only
50-100 Hold'em, can it? I'm still tired. No, I'm all right. This
is a perfect time to be up. Even if I feel like shit. I can do yoga
after I see what's happening. Better to get my chips down if
there's a good game going or get on a list first. I dry off with
two towels and take a third one to walk with until I decide
what to wear. I count the money laying on the night table. A
little over six thousand. And I've got seven thousand more in
my box downstairs. But I entered the Taj with seventeen
thousand on Wednesday. A thousand dollars for my right-
hand pocket and five for the money belt around my waist.

I enter the back door of the poker room, head straight for
the high-limit area. Come into the room feeling the adrenaline rush, looking for action. I bypass the 50-100 Hold'em on
my left because I see Louie's head at a table in the corner.
What's he up to?

Oh beauty. In the back corner there's a three-way game,
75-150. Porky and Louie and Floyd and Hurst from Amsterdam and Blue Ned and another fellow. They probably started
it up a little while after I went to bed. I sit right down. I'm
wearing my greet-'em-up suit, jeans with a zippered cotton
jacket, green and brown, hippieish. And a green Chinese army
cap and sunglasses. Always sunglasses.

I sit on Louie's left. He thinks I'm funny. Maybe because
he always seems to win when I'm in the game. He almost
always plays bad. Innocent like a child. Louie has two modes.
One when he's smoking Carltons, packs of disgusting card-
board filter air chemical no tar Carltons, and the other mode
when he's smoking his rubber cigarette. That's Louie for you.

He's won both days I've seen him play this trip. Stuck

around long enough to laugh 'em up. He loves the life. Everybody does when they're winning. This trip he's smoking on his rubber cigarette.

I buy in for a thousand dollars and get off to a rocky start. But I like to be here. The waitress swings by and I order a black coffee and a grapefruit juice. Insta-wake-up. The 50-100 Hold'em is still going in the center of the room, Captain Tom surveys all from his perch at the end of the table. Big Stud game broke some time ago and has yet to start up again. No sign of Jung.

I look around my table. Hurst is sitting on my left, and I'm none too excited about that young guy full of focus, always thinking, always playing good cards, always on the ball. But Floyd is in the game, playing like a man on fire, and Porky's in it and a guy I don't know and I'm thinking sooner or later it's gonna be a good game, as I go all in. Time for my first break. The next half hour is Stud Hilo and that's like my weakest game, anyway. Now I know what I'm up against.

I'm not really that upset. A thousand bucks goes like the wind in this game. It was Omaha Hilo and I got a couple of hands to play and they didn't turn out so well. Low never got there. Flush draw, dead on the river. But I'm only buying in for eight hundred from now on. If I'm gonna run bad then I'm gonna just last it out.

The Taj Mahal rules only state that you have to buy in for five times the maximum bet. In 75-150, that's only seven hundred and fifty dollars. You can play that money all in before you have to take out at least another seven-fifty. Some people like Jimmy, and me in the old days, don't worry about none of that shit. I just kept a lot of money on the table at all times because then no one knows if you're winning or losing.

You just look intimidating. And back then we'd never go all in. I thought it was a big disadvantage to be going all in all the time. Now I just think it helps the money last longer when you're losing. But I've had a lot more practice at losing than I used to.

Man, my neck hurts. This is a good time to do some yoga. And then smoke a joint. And think about how I'm gonna take these guys' money when it gets to Hold'em and what I should wear that's gonna freak 'em out. . . .

I slip back into my seat quietly, but it's hard to keep a straight face because Louie takes one look at me and almost has a convulsion. Man, is he goofy. He's bent over in his chair and looking for the rubber cigarette that he spit out when he started laughing and the shiny bald top of his head is staring right at me. I'm trying to look serious in my pink and green corduroy pants with an old-time cardigan, blue wool with brass buttons up the front and funny-looking ribbed pockets. My Ghanaian kebab hat, reggae colors. And the ghouly-eyed sunglasses.

Hurst don't know how to act toward me. "Everything all right?" he says gently.

Poker's about making decisions. And there's a lot of them to make because cards are coming and every time the action comes to you, you have to make a decision. Bet or fold. Call or raise. And making all those decisions second after second minute after minute hour after hour, can you see the infinite number of permutations there are of those decisions? And most of the time you never find out for sure if you're right or wrong because you don't get to see the cards or you don't show them or you didn't know what card was on top of the deck, and that's where the skill comes in. It's whoever makes the most number of decisions right. No, it's who ends up with all the cash. And there's the irony. They are definitely related but don't try and pin it down exactly.

Time to take another break. I leave my seventeen dollars in chips on the table and take a hike. Time for a new suit.

I NEVER REALLY saw the snow that weekend. I mean I heard about it and I watched it on TV and I saw white out my fiftieth-floor window at the Taj Mahal, but I never left the casino. And neither did anybody else.

It got real crazy. Just when the storm broke Saturday about daybreak and they were going to plow the roads, it started blizzarding again and a whole new lot dumped in. A total of twenty-four inches piled up in Atlantic City that weekend. The dealers couldn't go home and the dealers couldn't come in, so they just stayed, and while they stayed, they worked. So when I been in the same game fourteen hours, the same dealers keep coming in the box, but now some of their bow ties are getting undone and, man, they're looking like I feel and the Taj set up cots in all the ballrooms so the workers could have a place to sleep, and they had to give out free rooms to everybody stuck at the Taj Mahal, even the ones who went broke, 'cause they had no way home and what else could they do?

Everybody wearing the same clothes for three days straight like that Asian kid who never got out of his suit. Meanwhile,

I'd disappear up to my room whenever need be to put on something different. I guess I had him slammed in that department.

Nobody had anything else to do. And nobody had any place that they could go. And no one could go out and no one could come in. So we all just sat down there and played cards.

There's a lot of reasons to lose a hand, when you're in at the end. Sometimes you have the best hand and lose on the last card. Sometimes even though you have the worst hand, your odds of winning are enough so that being in is justified. Sometimes you think you have the best hand and you have the worst hand. And sometimes you just get so lost that you're just in and then you get out on a weird limb and just wind up scratching your head and staring at the ceiling when the hand is over. Whatever the reason, it's always the same. Nice hand, and on to the next one. Stack your remaining chips or take out more money. Or take a break to go get some more.

I'm sitting in my room and staring at the ceiling. I look at the clock and stare off into space again. Now I'm a little bit fuckin' pissed off, inhaling hard on a quickly made joint. I'm going for a different tactic. I'm gonna try and scare them out. I don't want no one calling no more when I bet. Ain't nobody raising me without the nuts. I put on my fake black leather pants and a black turtleneck. My black and dull pink knit cap. The Himalayan mirrored sunglasses. A scowl. Fuck them. I'm gonna go down and take some money. I stub out the joint and turn the air all the way up. Now's the time.

Oh man. I mean I'm sitting in my chair giving everyone the grumpy, when I play a hand shuffling around in my seat back and forward and in between a deal I slam my chips down and glower and look down and then I catch Hurst looking at me and I give him a smile. Guy doesn't know what to think, he knows me from Vienna where I was polite and talkative and didn't wear no sunglasses and played tight and accompanied him in winning the money. None of that shit going down in this game, me stuck about four thousand, but it looks like I'm down more—grouching around and all in five times, while Hurst in a zone like a wide-eyed demon and running through our three-way game like it's butter. Man, I wish he would leave, ain't no way he's gonna crack.

I peer out of the concrete jungle my mind is sitting in and check out the future of this game. I like it. There's ole Floyd scratching the wispy hair on his shiny head, body all tensed up, sitting forward, eyes going from the flop to his cards to the flop to the bettor. He's in like every hand. He's been winning a few pots lately and he's got good stacks of chips to go with the stack of hundreds that he counts like every five minutes, and every time someone puts a hundred in the pot Floyd is the first one to say, "Bring it over here," to change the bill into chips so he can figure out how much he's down again and count his hundreds for the twelfth time since this dealer's been in the box. He's on the comeback trail, OTC-ing, but he's stuck in his chair like a rat and ain't gonna leave until he gets even—play forever until he gets even. That's why I love to play with him. But he sure has gotten even plenty of times that I've seen. And then he's out of his seat so fast you'd think it caught fire.

In a typical game, you only see one or two players' hands every two or three deals. That leaves a lot of time for not really knowing what people are doing. Not knowing for absolutely sure. Just guessing by the way they act and when they throw their cards away and how often they throw their cards away. That's all. And whatever else comes to you, and there's always whatever else.

It ain't like I'm getting up every five minutes to go to my room. Some buy-ins last longer than others, and sometimes I double my stack through before I lose it and once I'm almost even for fifteen minutes or so. But there's no doubt as the session wears on that I'm losing, and my cards are rather gruesome. There's no flow. There's no order. Sometimes I go for an hour without playing more than a few hands, and then all of the sudden I get about ten to play in a row and get brutalized and then it's all over and I feel like a tornado went through my head and sucked up my chips and I'm just shell-shocked and thinking about all the hands while Louie and Porky are chortling. And then dry as a bone. Sit back and wait. And fume.

Sometimes I make a pledge like I'm gonna die right here in this seat rather than quit this game because it's so good. And don't it always seem to be that when you make the pledge, those are the days you really do sit there and just die in the seat. That's what it feels like. Just sitting there and dying, man.

Hurst has got so many chips he almost looks scared. Nobody else is winning in the game, except maybe Porky. I can't really tell, the man's got so many moves. In any case Porky ain't on tilt right now. He's sitting all back in his chair and he's got a calm smile for me and a private laugh about my clothes. What the hell am I saying, he's definitely ahead in the game. He must of just socked it away somewhere.

I see Jung standing behind the 50-100 Hold'em table, just woke up. He's talking to Captain Tom. Jung comes over to see if I want to play higher, if I'll help them start up a bigger

Hold'em game. Yeah, right. I've only got my thirteen hundred dollars in chips in front of me and then I've got to go to my box to get the remaining seven thousand. And Jung's all fresh, even though he is still wearing his tan suit. I guess he don't sweat much.

Jung and DB and Captain Tom and Poodles start up the 150-300 Hold'em anyway, four-handed. They set up at a table away from everything. I don't like the smell of it. I'm sticking it out here. I know I'm getting killed, but I ain't playing higher and it's not gonna be a better game than this one.

I know what it's like to be treated like the live one. It's easy to spot, especially if they ain't slick. And the guys beating me these days, they ain't slick at all, they ain't slicker than I was back a whole long time ago when I was rising and focused and star-struck and had a horseshoe up my ass just to roll into town with. Now they're waiting for me, they all want to play with me, snickering when I leave the table, and I guess so, I'm the guy throwing the party. But for who. A bunch of guys who will all go broke. Fuck. I ain't never giving my money to a guy like the Fresca Kid. He ain't giving no action. I want to be in with the guys who I know are going broke. Because then it's either them or me. And I really can't see where their big picture is at.

With that thought in mind, it takes me only three hands to lose the chips in front of me. The way they happened was like from a weird "This Is Your Life" show. Now I gotta go to my box and get some more money. I guess it's really more symbolically depressing than anything else. I sign my name and open the long box, empty but for a very outdated buffet comp and my seven thousand dollars. I leave the buffet comp.

What's going through my mind as I'm going through all that money, trudging back and forth from the poker room to my room, padding through the carpeted casino at all hours, at every hour. Sometimes I take the long way around, getting off on the second floor so I don't have to walk through the casino and weave between banks of slot machines. Instead I walk past closed boutiques and go down the escalator under the giant chandelier.

What's going through my mind. What's going through my mind is the same thing that's going through my mind when I'm sitting in a 20-40 Hold'em game at the Mirage when I haven't been in Vegas in a year and I haven't spent any real time there in five years and I haven't said one word to one player at the table and I've just raised six pots in a row and haven't gotten to show my hand even one time and an annoying bespectacled English bloke down the side of the table says, "Sir, you've used up your limit of pre-flop raises." To his little groupie enclave of ace-king buddies down at the other end of the table, day players and professionals with hourly win rates and computer analyses of every bet and triple-raised folds. And then when I just give him the stare he says, "And apparently he has no sense of humor, either."

What's going through my mind is, Man, you got all your money, your entire everything sitting in your front pocket and I know your deal cold like I know what you got, and I ain't been there in so long it's scary and I ain't never going back there again. I don't ever want to do that again. Done that. Did it before you ever knew what Hold'em was.

And then I'm thinking, and this guy, everybody at the table, thinks that I ain't even ready for that now, can't beat this scene, got no game. How scary is that? How strange does everything really seem? Either in poker everything is very illusory, or I'm pulling one giant hoax on myself.

All right. Now I'm getting desperate. I'm gonna have to pull out some of the big guns. I'm putting on my yellow pants. They are bright tight yellow sunflower pants with no pockets and a big wide white belt. My yellow and green button-down flower shirt. And a white captain's cap with a big brown spot on the top. This person is gonna win.

I don't really spend too much time taking stock of my situation up in the room. I mean it's nice to let the game stew, but I'm stuck too fuckin' big to do anything but get back down there and play. I just want to smoke another joint and come at 'em from a different angle. Pick myself up off the floor and give them a different look.

See, I feel like every time I come up to my room, it's a time I could be sitting at the table pissed off and on tilt. Instead I can be up in my room and take my time and get my thoughts together and get focused. But that's not the way it seems to end up happening. It seems to end up with me making a beeline for the room and strip down for a two-minute shower and watching the clock the whole time I make a quick joint and pick out some clothes that have got to be lucky and hurry back out the door to get down to the table by the time they change the game. It's just that I don't want to miss anything. I mean besides Hurst, ain't nobody doing nothing down there but gambling it up. It's just all so silly.

I look around the poker room. It's four o'clock in the afternoon and things have really picked up in here. The shift manager's beagle is running around loose. Dealers on break sit at empty tables with their collars undone and their feet propped up on unused chairs. Security guards are nonexistent. I'm playing thirteen hours in the same seat and now I'm wearing yellow pants and a flower-power shirt.

Two arms put some bills down in the empty seat on the other side of Louie and I look up and there's ET, and now I remember why he has his nickname. ET comes down from North Jersey to play Hold'em on the weekends, but I've known him since Foxwoods, when he used to drive to Connecticut on the weekends and he's always been the same. When he's even or winning, ET couldn't be a nicer guy. Or a more logical player. He's Woody Allen witty and always telling me the joke about the chicken sandwich.

When ET starts losing, something happens. First off he starts playing like every hand. And if he's not in the hand, he's there anyway, I swear he looks like ET, moving from a long thin neck, eyes bugged out and dilated to about three times their size, always jerky, moving that neck over the table to look at the flop, at the bettor, back at his cards, his hands throwing out chips. And he'll just go like that until he gets even. Or until he wins a few pots in a row and manages to grab ahold of himself for a while. But I've never seen him play anything but Hold'em, and rarely higher than 50-100. What's happening? What happened to the 50-100 Hold'em?

I turn around and it all becomes clear. When Poodles and Captain Tom left to start the big Hold'em, the 50-100 game began to crumble. Those nits don't like to play short-handed anyway. So now the game's just broke and they're all going to bed, except for ET who's stuck and ain't going anywhere. But he's not playing 150-300, that's way too high for him, so he comes over to our game, I mean we are playing thirty minutes of Hold'em every hour and a half. And we are trapped in a casino during a snowstorm.

ET comes into the game on tilt. He plays the first hand, asks, "This is eight or better for low, right?" Calls all the way to the end, gets half the pot using an eight-six from his hand for low, plays the next hand, loses, and man, he is strapped in.

I guess you can't really understand tilt well unless you've been there. But every poker player has been there. Every gambler. My favorite Mr. Boffo cartoon says the definition of temptation is constructing the most scientifically advanced computerized horse racing handicapping program known to man and then finding out that there's a horse in the third race with the same birthday as your dog.

Tilt is when all the rules you made for yourself, all the order that you have in the casino—it doesn't matter if it's real or not, it's your order—all that goes out the window and what you're left with is a burning desire to get even and a more burning desire to get in action. That's tilt, and that's when most people lose most of their money. Oh sure, there's something that comes before, like when your set of kings get beat by a back-door flush or you lose with four big pairs inside of a half hour or you lose a big pot because the guy next to you raised with nothing or whatever, there's always something that puts you on tilt. And you might remember that as the reason you lost. But once you're there, man, most guys are like ET with the bug eyes and up over the table and in every hand and making sudden motions and moving around a million miles a minute and money in and money out and it's to the maximum. When I play with people and they're acting like that, it sure is hard to believe that they can make better

decisions than me, that they can win. But they do. I mean
sometimes. I mean here I am. Does that mean I'm good or
does that mean I'm bad? Or do we have to find out the end of
the story.

What's happening is clouded, clouded because no one
knows for sure and clouded because I want to cloud it. I want
everyone to think I'm some rich trust-fund baby who has land
in Golan Heights and just rolls in money, I want them to
think I just wear outlandish clothes because I'm really crazy
and don't care about nothing but being crazy, I want them to
think that I lose all the time. And now look at me sitting here.
Look at me sitting here high as a gourd thinking I'm the best
player and all I've done since I got back from Asia is dump
money, cash money, in other people's pockets. With almost no
positive encouragement except for fleeting inner order. Fleeting, as in comes and goes. Depending on who won the hand.
But I'm only gonna find that feeling in the game.

I peer around and check out the status of my table. Poor
Louie has taken the worst of it lately. But who didn't know
that was gonna happen sooner or later, old two-year-old sucking his fuckin' pacifier rubber cigarette. You think that guy
doesn't have gambling in his blood? Man, he is all addiction.

Hurst is racking his chips and I stare with amazement at
the stack of cash he had concealed under his stacks. I hadn't
realized he was up so much. It looks like he's quitting. I can't
believe it. How can you quit this spot? Well, I guess if I'd been
playing seventeen hours and was ahead like nine thousand,
then I'd quit the game, too. Last year we were in the same
Hold'em game in Vienna. Same players. Now look at us.

Blue Ned's looking pretty ready to go also. He was dozing
before, but now he's beat in his seat, just trying to get his last

eight hundred in chips into action so he can lie on a real bed.
If he doesn't go on a big rush now, then he's done for. He
seems to be running like me lately.

Oh, my God, Floyd is even. He's laughing and sitting back
and holy cow, he's even standing up to stretch his legs. I can't
believe he got even. It must've been the last hand with ET
that did it. Heck, he was stuck four dimes when I got in the
game, now I realize he's only playing two more hands, just
waiting for his blind. He's gonna go. That must be why Hurst
is leaving. I hadn't even realized Floyd had stopped playing
bad and started folding hands. How out of it am I?

I got a big fog in my head and I feel like I'm being made to
walk through the circle of death. I've been in the game since
three in the morning and with the exception of the unknown
busting out around 8 A.M., no one moved in thirteen hours.
Now everything seems to happen all in a row. ET sits down.
Floyd and Hurst and Blue Ned quit. And I go all in again.
Now I'm stuck almost eight dimes in this piece-of-shit game. I
give Louie's cards a long stare and then him a cold level look,
he just giggles and looks down and then looks at me quick and
then away and says, "Well, I mean I was going for a straight."
Giggles again. I place my cards face down into the muck and
the dealer pushes Louie the pot and I push my chair back and
say I'll be right back and walk out of the poker room without
looking back.

Everybody wants to win. No, I mean poker players want to
stay in action, and to stay in action you have to win. Everybody talks about the money, what they're gonna do with it
and this and that and I've never met the man but I respect the
hell out of Stu Ungar because when he won the World Series

and he was asked, "What are you gonna do with the money?" he giggled and said, "Blow it." Now apparently this is a guy who likes action and everyone's always talking about what assholes the rich guys are and all the guys standing on the rail of the big game are saying, I wish I had that money. But they don't want the money, they want the action, and they're thinking, If I had it I'd just play and play as long and whenever I want to. Because they're standing on the rail out of action in that bells-ringing and lights-whirring casino and they need that fuckin' adrenaline rush. Hey, man, I been in action since I was sixteen and I think it's just about taken my heart away because all of the sudden the road is lit up in lights and I can see down it and I know what's down there. Today I don't feel so special.

I mean everybody in that room is the same, man, I seen it happen. Fuckin' poker took the world by storm, it rode into town on a wave sometime in the eighties, and poker was fun and money was everywhere and games were everywhere and we didn't know how to play but we learned a little and for some reason most of us won. And the ones who didn't win went broke and left the scene and we called them bad players and went on and, man, the circle shrinking and shrinking and you say to yourself, Hah! That guy went broke—you see? He didn't know what the fuck poker is about and as long as guys like him are around I'll never go broke.

But what really happened? Poker is clouded by more shrouds of mystery than the Holy Bible because now it's a few years later and I'm sitting with the same guys. I mean they got different faces and accents and all but I'm sitting with 'em and now they take all my money and laugh loudly at my expense and say how as long as I'm around they'll never go broke. And now after five years of the silver platter life on wheels, harsh reality is you gotta fuckin' be like everyone else.

I know it's all coming down to that suit. I mean everything about the suit was like weird destiny. Like when Sy Tan the tailor had leftover material from the four meters of royal purple English cashmere that I found in a stall at the old Saigon market. So he made an extra pair of pants with twelve-inch bell-bottom cuffs. That suit fit me like pajamas, strutting around in his tailor shop that doubled as a home for him and his wife and their six or seven children in downtown Saigon. Everyone staring at me and the looks on their faces, and if I looked weird there, then what about a million miles away in Atlantic City with the addition of a Nepalese Dr. Seuss three-foot purple velvet thingamabob hat.

All right. Get it together, man. Now they're all playing really bad. Now it's a zoo down there. Put on the suit and play good and gotta get even. Gotta just get some money back. Now's the time to get some money. It better be.

I just feel like I want to cry. I been walking back and forth from my room to the table changing my clothes and taking out more money and everybody's laughing at me and calling me a fool and forget that, do I think I'm a fool? Am I being foolish. They think they are going to beat me. And they do. I think I'm going to win and I don't. And I still think I'm playing okay. Or I know how to play okay. Or I know how to play sort of sometimes brilliant. Or I'm getting better. Or whatever. I just don't buy them beating me given what I know and yet they do and I'm still changing my clothes and telling myself that I'm fooling them. I'm riding down in the elevator staring into the mirror and telling the guy in the sunglasses that he's fooling them. Go get 'em.

The purple suit caused a little bit of a stir. But they didn't stop the game. Not really. The place is a fuckin' zoo anyway. Everybody wanted to wear the hat, but I wouldn't let them. Not at first. Let's see if they can concentrate on the game. I can. I think.

You gotta understand what it is. I mean I'm sitting there high as a kite looking through my one-way glasses and I'm watching them watch me. Watching them. Watch me. You see I'm really watching them, but what are they watching. Is it me? I don't even know anymore, and in that big bright casino where the dealers wear bow ties and the cocktail waitresses prance around in minis and money is colored chips and people's eyes are glazed and bells are ringing, I don't know what level I'm on. I just know that I crossed a line somewhere. With my whiller wham 'em hat. See, because I've convinced myself I'm focused.

Eight trips to the room. Eight new outfits. Eight thousand dollars gone. And the two guys I'm losing to are ET and Louie. The world I'm in is much stranger than my purple hat. But Louie's giving me the big laugh, a ho ho ho, and sucking on his rubber cigarette, that big silly kid's grin spreading wide his whole face. I mean, I've gotta be the only guy this man has ever beat, and he always wins when I'm in the game.

Yeah, ET's on tilt. And Louie's on tilt. Just like Floyd before them, and I think, Now's the time I'm gonna win some money.

I don't know what happened to the next three thousand. Sometimes money burns faster than you can throw it out of

your hands. I didn't win any pots for a while. Maybe picked
up the blinds a few times. ET wins twenty-five hundred or
three thousand all of the sudden and then Hold'em is over
and he's gone. Another guy I got even. Porky plays for another half hour just because it's Seven Stud Hilo and then
Louie ain't even really down so much anymore, but we agree
to play head up just for a little while.

I've got him beat cold. I've got him beat fuckin' red cold. I
mean I couldn't beat six, five, four, or three, but now when it's
just me and Louie left, I got the nuts. And I start torturing
him. Just when I've got him stuck about two thousand in
thirty minutes of head up, he wins it all back in about four or
five consecutive huge hands and he's out of there.

I'm left sitting alone at the table. Big loser. I want to keep
playing and they all quit me. I guess that's the only end for
this nightmare. I feel like I'm dead in the chair.

BACK IN AMSTERDAM, first man on the ground. That's
what Morty said and it immediately sticks in my head like
one of those W.W.II paratroopers, our man on the ground in
France. It sure is tough finding action in this town, games that
can be beat.

I bust into the Holland casino just before 2 A.M. so I don't
have to play for more than an hour or so at the murderous 5
percent no-cap limit poker in which there is no way for anyone to ever win in the long run except for the house and quite

hard to win in the short run. Morty, after toying with the idea for a while, getting up after about four hours and declaring, "You can have my seat, Mickey. I'm about even. The rest of the money's in the till. I fail to see the point." But I'm only there trying to get people to go over to the twenty-four-hour Concord Card Club that just opened outside of town. The rake is lower, but it's empty, nobody goes there.

Morty and I did get a whole bunch of people to go to the Concord that night. After the government casino closed at 3 A.M., Michael gave us a ride out of town, a long quiet ride in the middle of the night in the back of his Renault, like driving in an old rusted sardine can or something. Nine guys showed up at the Concord—they were flabbergasted to see us roll in at three-thirty in the morning, and it wasn't long before free drinks were flowing and hot hors d'oeuvres. They made us breakfast and we had a righteous old game for a few hours until these guys drifted back into the woodwork, a shame because they couldn't play a lick. Paul, Michael, and a host of Asians. Build it and they will come.

Walking into that poker room was funny, because there they are in the middle of nowhere in a fuckin' industrial park outside of town. And I know it's gonna be a hit, just know it, know it like I can see the future. Like I've seen what happened in Foxwoods and AC and Vienna and now I'm the man on the ground and I'm gonna take my cut.

Or something. The next night I'm back at the government-owned Holland casino, playing in the small game, 10-20 dealer's choice, when an old man from Belgium sitting in the corner asks the dealer, "This game ends at three? So what do we do from three till six o'clock?" And I knew I had my first target. A little while later I've got this man ready to come with me in a taxi to the Concord to try and start a game. Our game breaks up at two forty-five and I've managed to only lose about three hundred guilders or so.

The 20-40 game is still rocking, sick people trying to squeeze one last hand out of a game with a 5 percent chop. A young fellow in the one seat, jeans and light hair, gets up and comes over to me. "Are you maybe interested in a private Pot-Limit game after this? That's where we're all going."

"I want to go to the Concord," I say, "and start up a game over there."

"No one's there."

"Well, is this game safe?"

"We all go over together," he says. I muttered something underneath my breath, he studied the lines on my face. Well, shit. Action is action and I might as well find out what's going on in this town. And since the locals had managed to talk the old guy into going with them, I trooped on over. There are about six of us and we walk through the center of town, down a few alleys, knock on a plain door, up a flight of stairs and into a very nicely furnished little club complete with a blackjack table and a big baccarat table nicely outfitted for poker. All Chinese guys lounging about. Good coffee. And fresh fruit slices and sandwiches and the waitress is there with a flick of your hand.

Hong runs the game. I'm locked up in a pretty big pot with him and I got two queens and I'm almost sure I got the best hand. Almost sure, and Hong makes a bet the size of the pot, about fifteen hundred guilders and there's still one card to come. I'm ahead pretty good in the game and the game's almost over and I'm thinking about it like this. If I lose the pot, I ain't gonna be happy. But if I win the pot, if I win the pot how much am I gonna like it? How am I gonna like beating the club owner for all his chips? How am I gonna like having all the money in a strange town in a mobster's private club where the door's locked and I don't know anybody and there ain't no guarantee of anything? So I think awhile, and then I say to Hong, "I'm gonna pass, I can't stand the heat."

And he flips over a bluff and points to the cards and says in a soft voice, "Control . . . it's all about control." Meaning like he's talking about cards and position and stuff like that. But I got another meaning. And I got out of there fast. And I don't feel bad about folding no winner neither.

I mean this guy Hong has got it made. And he knows it, smart fuckin' dude watches his game like a hawk, knows exactly what's going on, ain't one to hang in the background. It shows he cares and it's one of his main things and who the fuck could blame him when you're talking about 5 percent chop and no one can fuckin' play. I mean I'm on the button in Pot-Limit Hold'em and there's a twenty-five-dollar live blind out and the action goes call call call fold call to me. I mean really.

It ain't like there's no money in Amsterdam, but it's too dangerous. The games are privately run and if I want my cut I gotta take it from the man. And he ain't no patsy. No. Hong might not play poker but he's one smart dude and has that game under his thumb and all the players in it and he's a strong arm and some kind of crime boss and I don't want no part of it, and when the game ended and I'm big winner and I should have won about three times as much I say, "Thanks for letting me play," and, "Does this game go all the time?" And Hong smiles and says, "Sorry, we only have this game on Fridays and Saturdays," and he's only smiling with his mouth.

His eyes are hard hard hard and I say, "Well, if I'm back in town sometime I'll be sure and come back," to which he says nothing just gives me the same smile. And when I get back to my hotel room I think that the next time I go back, if I'm big winner I could be in big trouble. Because Hong wants all the money, and he knows he'll get it, too, at 5 percent chop, as long as no one plays too good. So long, boys, I'm headed for Austria.

THERE'S NOT MANY people who get it. My friend Wolf- gang does, though. We see each other about once or twice a year at some random European event, either in Salzburg or Vienna or Bregenz. And about eight in the morning when all the big games just broke up and all the players are standing around the bar drinking heavy and chatting up the cashier girls and waitresses who just got off shift, Wolfgang looks at me from across the room and says in a loud voice with his German accent, "Mickey, you still got any money?"

And I say, "YES!!" And I put my fist in the air, and then we give each other a mental high five and break up laughing all over the place. And everyone just stares. You see, they don't get it. Because that's all that's important. It's the only thing.

bitterness and denial aren't
realistic ways
to deal
with something that happens again and again
never to know exactly when
but that the only stop is not to play.
but to play
that's the thing.
shut up and deal.